More things he shouldn't be doing...

He shouldn't be wrapping his arms around Steph and pulling her close. Shouldn't be finding the taste of her even sweeter than he'd dared to imagine.

Shouldn't be. But he was.

He pulled her up and into him.

Wrong, he thought. But that didn't stop him. And she didn't seem to mind. Far from it—she kissed him right back. He didn't want it ever to end.

But he knew it had to. Exerting a superhuman effort, he lifted his mouth from hers. There was a moment, and they stared at each other.

"I'm sorry," he said. "I don't know what the hell my problem is. I shouldn't have done that."

And Steph smiled a smile that became so bright it blinded him. "Oh, yeah," she said. "You should have. And I'm real glad you did."

Dear Reader,

In Thunder Canyon, Montana, big changes are taking place. A modern-day gold rush and a fabulously successful new resort have signaled sudden prosperity and growth in the picturesque mountain town.

Ex-rancher Grant Clifton is having the time of his life, making money hand over fist, doing work he loves. Beautiful women flock to him. His life is just the way he'd never dared to dream it might be. It's perfect….

Until the day he finally sees Steph Julen—the girl next door, his honorary little sister—as the grown woman she's somehow become. Sparks fly and all hell breaks loose when the man who has everything realizes there's something missing in his life, after all: love. It's not what he planned on, not what he bargained for.

Too bad. Steph is one determined cowgirl and she's out to get her man.

Yours,

Christine Rimmer

CHRISTINE RIMMER

THE MAN WHO HAD EVERYTHING

Silhouette®

SPECIAL EDITION®

Published by Silhouette Books

America's Publisher of Contemporary Romance

Special thanks and acknowledgment are given to Christine Rimmer for her contribution to the MONTANA MAVERICKS: STRIKING IT RICH miniseries.

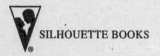

SILHOUETTE BOOKS

ISBN-13: 978-0-373-24837-7
ISBN-10:   0-373-24837-7

THE MAN WHO HAD EVERYTHING

Copyright © 2007 by Harlequin Books S.A.

Visit Silhouette Books at www.eHarlequin.com

Printed in U.S.A.

CHRISTINE RIMMER

came to her profession the long way around. Before settling down to write about the magic of romance, she'd been everything, including an actress, a salesclerk and a waitress. Now that she's finally found work that suits her perfectly, she insists she never had a problem keeping a job—she was merely gaining life experience for her future as a novelist. Christine is grateful not only for the joy she finds in writing, but also for what waits when the day's work is through: a man she loves, who loves her right back, and the privilege of watching their children grow and change day to day. She lives with her family in Oklahoma. Visit Christine at her new home on the Web at www.christinerimmer.com.

For all you Montana Mavericks fans.
You are the very best!

Chapter One

Grant Clifton set out that sunny Sunday afternoon with the best of intentions.

He meant for Stephanie Julen and her mom, Marie, to know of his plans good and early, so they could start getting used to the idea. He had it all laid out in his mind, just how he'd tell them.

First, he would remind them that you can't hold on to the past forever. That sometimes you've got to let go of what used to be, let the wave of progress and prosperity take you. Dump the excess baggage and move on.

In his own life, Grant was doing exactly that. And loving every minute of it. He would make

Steph and Marie understand that it was time for them to move on, too.

Since the sun was shining bright and proud in the wide Montana sky, Grant called down to the stables and had one of the grooms tack up Titan, the big black gelding he rode whenever he got the chance—which wasn't all that often lately. He worked behind a desk now. His days as a rancher were behind him.

In his private suite of rooms on-site at the Thunder Canyon Resort, he changed into Wranglers and boots and a plain blue chambray shirt. When he got to the stables, Titan was ready to go. The gelding whickered in greeting and tossed his fine black head, eager to be off. The groom loaned Grant a spare hat and he grinned to himself as he rode out.

A Clifton without a battered straw Resistol close at hand to stave off the glare of the summer sun? His dad would never approve.

Fact was, John Clifton probably wouldn't have approved of a lot of things lately. Too bad. Grant settled the hat lower on his brow and refused to let his grin fade as he let Titan have his head and the horse took off at a gallop.

On Titan's strong back, the ride to the house at Clifton's Pride Ranch took about an hour. Once he'd left the sprawling resort behind, Grant rode cross-country, stopping now and then to open a gate, going back and closing it once his horse went through.

In the distance, the high mountains still bore their white caps. And the grasses, which would be fading to gold soon enough, lay green and lush beneath the gelding's hooves, rippling in the ever-present Montana wind.

As Titan ambled up and down the cuts and draws, Grant rehearsed what he would say. Yeah, he knew Steph and her mom would be disappointed. But he would remind them that he would always take care of them. He would make sure they had work when they left the ranch. That much would never change: He would watch out for them.

In no time, it seemed, he reached Clifton land.

He took a couple of dirt roads he knew of and then approached another pasture gate, patiently shutting it behind him once his horse went through. A few cows, lying down near the fence, got up from their grassy bed and looked at him expectantly. He tipped his borrowed hat at them, mounted up again and rode on.

Ahead, cottonwoods loomed, lush and green, lining the banks of Cottonwood Creek. They seemed taller and thicker than he remembered, obscuring the creek completely now. Grant clicked his tongue and urged the horse onward, his mind on getting it over with, getting Steph and her mom together and breaking the news that he'd had a great offer and he was selling Clifton's Pride.

The horse mounted a grassy slope and carried him in beneath the screen of wind-ruffled trees, where the ground was mossy and soft and Titan's hooves hardly made a sound. Grant could smell water, hear the soft gurgling of the creek not far ahead. He topped another slight rise and the creek lay below, crystal clear and inviting.

But it wasn't the sight of the creek that stole the breath from Grant Clifton's lungs.

He drew on the reins without thinking. Soundlessly Titan came to a stop.

A woman stood at creekside. A naked woman. Beads of water gleamed on her golden skin and her hair, clinging in soaked tendrils to her shoulders, dripped a shining wet trail down the center of her slim, straight back.

She faced the opposite bank. As he stared, she lifted both hands and smoothed her hair, cupping the delicate shape of her skull, catching the wet strands at her nape, wringing gently, so that more water trickled in little gleaming trails along that amazing back, between those two little dimples that rode the base of her spine…

Grant's gaze followed the path of the water. Sweet Lord. The lower he looked, the harder he lusted. He sat frozen in place astride the gelding, feeling the blood pool hot in his groin, his pulse pounding so deep and hungry and loud, he was surprised the woman didn't hear it and turn.

What the hell was she doing there, naked beneath the cottonwoods on Clifton land?

Not that he planned to ask. Not right now.

He would have smiled—if only if he hadn't been aching so bad with desire. Make no mistake. He'd find out who she was one way or another. He'd get to know her. Well.

But now would probably be a bad time to introduce himself.

Light as a breath, he laid the reins to Titan's neck. The horse started to turn—and the woman raised her slim arms to the sky and let out a laugh, a sound all at once free and husky and glorious.

His mind reeled. He knew that laugh.

Steph's laugh.

Grant drew the horse up short again.

Impossible.

This beautiful, naked stranger, fully a woman… *Steph?*

His head spun with denials. Stephanie Julen was hardly more than a kid, she was like a little sister to him, she was…

Twenty-one.

Damn it. Couldn't be. No way.

The woman who couldn't be Steph laughed again, and then, without warning, in midlaugh, she turned.

And she saw him there, frozen in place, at the top of the bank. The green eyes that always looked at him with trust and admiration widened in shock as she formed his name on a low cry.

"Grant?" Frantic, she tried to cover herself, one

hand to her small, perfect breasts, the other to the patch of dark gold curls between her smooth, amazing thighs. "Oh, God…"

At least he had the presence of mind to lay the reins at the horse's neck again and, that time, to follow through.

Once he faced the way he'd come, he called over his shoulder, "Get dressed." He kept his voice as calm and level as possible, given his own stunned, disbelieving state of arousal. "Ride on back to the house with me…"

Behind him, she was dead silent—except for a low, agonized groan.

"Come on." He kept his gaze resolutely front and he forced all hint of gruffness from his tone. "It's okay." He spoke gently. Soothingly. "I'm sorry I…surprised you."

Behind him, down the bank, he heard frenzied rustling sounds as she scrambled to get into her clothes. He waited, taking slow breaths, knowing he had to be calm and unruffled, totally unconcerned, in order to put her at ease again.

At ease. Damn. Didn't he wish?

Within a couple of minutes that only *seemed* to last for eternity, he heard the soft thuds of hooves behind him. She came up beside him mounted on her favorite mare, Trixiebelle.

Unbelievable. He'd been so busy gaping at her naked backside and planning how he would get her into his bed, he hadn't even noticed she had her horse down there by the creek with her.

Titan chuffed in greeting and Trixiebelle snorted a response.

Grant put on a smile and turned it on Steph, not allowing it to waver, even as another bolt of lust went zinging through him.

Her clothes were as wet as the rest of her. Her shirt clung to the fine, sleek curves he'd never noticed till moments ago—curves that from this afternoon onward would remain seared into his brain.

Impossible. Wanting Steph. It had to be illegal. Or, at the very least, immoral.

Didn't it?

Her hair hung in damp ropes on her shoulders and her sweet, innocent face was flaming red. "How long were you…" Her voice faltered. She swallowed and made herself finish. "…watching me?"

"I wasn't," he baldly lied, somehow managing to keep his easy smile in place at the same time. "I'd just topped the rise when you saw me." He turned Titan again and started down the bank to creekside. She followed.

Since she would know the best place to cross, he pulled back once they reached the bank and signaled her to take the lead.

All too aware of the man behind her, Steph rode Trixiebelle into the shallows. Once on the other side, they climbed the far bank and emerged from under the dappling shade of the cottonwoods into open pasture. Grant caught up with her and rode at her side.

She didn't look at him. She couldn't bear to meet his eyes right yet—and if only her silly cheeks would stop blushing.

Really. It wasn't *that* big a deal.

Okay, it was embarrassing. Way embarrassing. She'd never in a million years expected Grant to appear on horseback out of nowhere during the rare moment she'd chosen to indulge herself in a quick, *private* skinny-dip.

He had to know she hadn't expected him—or anyone, for that matter—didn't he?

After all, he hardly ever came to the ranch anymore. In the six months since he'd hired her to take over the job of foreman, this was the first time she'd seen him out on the land. As a rule, when he did drop by, he always stuck to the roads and arrived at the ranch house in that fancy black Range Rover of his.

Grant didn't have time for the ranch these days. He was too busy at the resort. In two short years, he's gone from sales associate to comanager. And he played as hard as he worked. Not a lot of nights went by that he didn't have some new out-of-town beauty hanging on his arm. The women loved him. He was thirty-two, single and getting rich fast.

Steph dared to slide him a glance. He was looking straight ahead.

He was also way too handsome. Always had been. His profile could take a girl's breath away: that sculpted nose, that fine mouth, that firm jaw. He was six foot four, lean, rangy and muscular—all at the same time. She had no doubt he'd seen a lot of naked women. To him, a naked female wouldn't be anything new.

She felt a stab of pure green jealousy as she thought of all those beautiful women he dated. Stephanie had loved Grant Clifton with all of her yearning heart since she was five years old. Of course, she knew he would never return her love. He cared for her. A lot. But not in *that* way.

And she was okay with that…

Or so she kept telling herself.

And what do you know? She wasn't blushing anymore. Her heart had stopped jumping around in her chest like a spooked jackrabbit and her pulse had even slowed a tad. Maybe hopeless blazing jealousy had its uses, after all.

So all right. He'd seen her naked. Best to get over it. Let it go. Move on.

But for some idiotic reason, she couldn't stop herself from launching into a totally lame explanation. "Me and Rufus pulled a cow out of that pond in the far pasture…"

Rufus Dale had been the top hand on Clifton's

Pride for as long as Steph could remember. He'd stepped up to run things when Grant started working at the resort. But arthritis had forced the old cowboy to slow down *and* given Steph her chance to take over for him.

She babbled on, "I sent him on back to the bunkhouse. You know how he gets these days. He hates that he can't do all the things that used to be so easy for him."

Grant didn't say anything. He didn't look at her, either. Was he mad at her, after all, for being out there in the altogether where anyone could ride up on her?

She tried again. "I was covered in mud. I got to the creek and it was just too darn tempting. I jumped in with my clothes on, to rinse everything off at once and, well, then I was all soggy—like now." She cast a rueful glance down at her wet shirt and jeans. "And it's a warm day and I couldn't help thinking how *good* the water would feel without… uh. Well, you know."

He grunted. Didn't he? Hadn't that been a grunt she heard?

"Uh, Grant?"

A grunt. A definite grunt. One with sort of a question mark at the end of it.

"I really didn't expect anyone to ride by. I truly didn't…"

"Steph."

She gulped. "Yeah?"

A pause. Her dread increased. Was he irritated? Amused? What? She just couldn't tell.

Then he actually looked at her again and gave her one of those gorgeous heartbreaker smiles of his. "Don't sweat it, okay? I know the feeling."

She felt her mouth bloom wide in a giant smile. "You do?" God. She sounded like such a dumb, innocent kid...

But he was nice about it. He was *always* nice. "Oh, yeah. Nothin' like a cold, clear creek on a hot day."

She clicked her tongue at Trixiebelle, who was showing more interest in cropping grass than in moving it along. "Well," she said, and couldn't think of a single clever thing to say. She finished lamely, "Good..."

They rode in silence the rest of the way. Stephanie tried to concentrate on the beauty of the green, rolling land around them and not to think about how he really must be irritated with her no matter how hard he tried to ease her embarrassment. He was so quiet, so reluctant to turn her way.

Bart, the old spotted hound, came out to meet them when they got to the house. He wiggled in delight, whining for attention from his old master.

Grant dismounted and took a moment to greet him, "There's a good boy." He gave the dog a nice scratch behind the ear.

Rufus emerged from the tack room as they

walked their horses into the barn. He shook Grant's hand in greeting and then started giving orders.

"Go on in the house, you two. Leave the horses to me. I'm still good for a few things around here, you know."

So they thanked him and headed across the open dirt yard to the plain, white-shingled, two-story house. On the wide front porch, Steph paused to pull off her muddy boots.

Inside, the old wood floors had a warm scuffed gleam and a short walk through the front hall past the simple oak staircase led them to the kitchen in back.

Marie Julen had the oven door open. She pulled a sheet of cookies out and set it on a rack to cool. And then she turned, her face breaking into a welcoming grin at the sight of Grant. "Well, look what the cat drug in."

Grant grinned. "Sure does smell good in here."

"Get over here, you."

In two long strides, he was across the room, grabbing Steph's mom in a hug. When he pulled back, he held her by her plump shoulders. "You bake those cookies just for me?"

She grinned up at him. "Well, of course I did—even though I had no idea at all that you were coming to visit today." She sent Steph a knowing look, taking in her soggy clothes and wet hair. "I'm guessing that cow is now safely out of the pond."

Steph nodded. "And I really need a shower—hey!" She faked a warning look at Grant, who'd already grabbed a couple of cookies. "Leave some for me."

"I'm makin' no promises." He winked at her when he said it and she dared to hope that the awkwardness between them was past.

She turned for the stairs as her mom tempted him with her fine cooking. "Pot roast for dinner."

Stephanie's heart lifted as she heard him answer, "Sounds too good to pass up. I'll stay."

Grant was downright relieved when Steph went upstairs.

He needed a little time to collect himself, to get used to the idea that she'd somehow grown up right under his nose, to get over his shock at how damn beautiful she was.

How could she have changed so much, so fast? Shouldn't he have noticed she was becoming a woman—a beautiful woman—before now?

He needed to stop thinking about her. He needed to remember his purpose here today. It wasn't going to be easy, telling them about the sale.

But then again, now he'd said he'd stay for dinner, there was no big rush to get into it. He'd break the news during the meal. That way Rufus and the other hand, Jim Baylis, would be there, too. He could tell them all at once, answer whatever questions they had right then and there, *and* reassure them that he'd find other work for all of them.

Steph already gave riding lessons at the resort, by appointment only. He was thinking he could get her something full-time at the stables. And maybe he could arrange to get Marie something where there would be cooking involved. Not at the resort, but possibly in town. She did love to cook and she was damn good at it, too.

He washed his hands in the sink and took a seat at the kitchen table. Marie, as usual, read his mind.

"Beer?"

"You bet."

She set the frosty bottle in front of him and then went back to the oven to take a peek at the other sheet of cookies she had baking in there. A born ranch wife, Marie loved taking care of the house and keeping the hands fed and happy. When she was needed, she would get out with the rest of them and drive cattle to higher summer pastures or work the chutes at branding time.

As he watched her bustling about, he couldn't help comparing mother to daughter. Steph had inherited Marie's light hair and green eyes, but she'd got her height and build from her dad. Andre Julen had been as tall and lean as Marie was short and round.

When Grant was growing up, the Julens had owned and worked the next ranch over, the Triple J. Marie and Grant's mom, Helen, were the best of friends. So were Andre and John. Grant's sister, Elise, and Steph used to play together, running up and down the stairs, giggling and whispering little-girl secrets while their mothers sat at the table where Grant sat now. Marie and Helen would drink strong black coffee and share gossip while they did the mending or snapped the beans for dinner.

Helen and Elise Clifton lived in Billings now. They'd signed over control of the ranch to him, though they still shared in any profits—including the big windfall that would come with the sale. His mom and sister seemed happy in Billings.

Marie and Steph, though....

For them, losing the Triple J six years ago had been like losing a husband and a father all over again. They were ranch folk to the bone....

"I heard that resort of yours is full up for the Fourth of July." Marie put the lid back on the cast-iron pot.

The Fourth was three days away, on Wednesday. Grant tipped his beer at Marie. "You bet we are." Teasing her, he quoted from a recent brochure. "Treat yourself to magnificent mountain views, sumptuous luxury, and thrilling recreation at Thunder Canyon Resort." He brought his beer to his heart and really hammed it up. "You've come to us for the best in winter sports and entertainment. Now, you're invited to explore our winding mountain trails, weaving in and out of lush forests, dotted with cascading streams." He paused, dramatically, then announced, "Thunder Canyon Resort. The ultimate vacation or conference spot—peaceful, refreshing, with an endless variety of activities. Come to relax. Come to party. We offer fun and excitement, rejuvenation of mind, body and soul in a majestic setting, year-round."

Marie laughed and clapped her hands and joked, "Sign me up."

He shrugged. "I admit, after Independence Day, things'll slow down. But hey. We're doing all right—and Marie, you've got to quit calling it *my* resort." Grant did have shares in the partnership, but the resort had started out as the dream child of the most powerful family in the area, the Douglases.

"They're lucky to have you working with them," Marie declared, loyal as the second mom she'd always been to him.

He thought about the sale of the ranch again. And hated himself a little. But he'd made his decision. He was never coming back here and neither were his mom or Elise. For the old man's sake, he'd given Clifton's Pride his best shot, but he wasn't a rancher and he never would be. Better to get out while a great offer was dangling right in front of his nose.

Marie added, "Everyone knows it was your idea to keep the resort open year-round. 'Nother beer?"

Grant thanked her, but decided to stroll on out to the barn and have a few words with Rufus instead.

The grizzled cowboy sat on a bale of hay, his hat

beside him, rolling a cancer stick in those stiff, knobby hands of his.

"Try not to burn the barn down while you're killin' yourself with that thing," Grant advised.

Rufus only grunted and stuck the rolled cigarette behind his ear. "You leavin' already? I just took the saddle off your horse." Stiffly, shaking his gray head, he started to rise.

Grant waved him back down. "I'm staying for dinner."

"Smart thinkin'. That Marie, she can cook." Rufus nodded sagely as he settled back on the bale. "Pot roast, I hear."

"That is the rumor…"

The old cowboy took the cigarette from behind his ear, shook his head at it and stuck it back there without lighting it. "She's doin' just fine, in case you wanted to know."

Grant knew exactly who *she* was. But for some reason he refused to examine too closely, he played it dumb. "Who? Marie?"

"No," Rufus said with great patience. "Not Marie. I mean little Stephanie—who ain't so little as she used to be, in case you didn't notice."

Grant ordered the image of her glorious bare backside to get the hell out of his mind and played it noncommittal with a deceptively easy shrug. "Yeah. Seems like only yesterday she was running around the yard in pigtails."

"She's a born rancher, that gal. Works hard. Loves every minute of it. And smart as a whip. You keep her on as top hand, I got a feeling she'll shock us all and make this ranch a profitable operation."

Clifton's Pride turning a profit?

Now, that *would* be an accomplishment. Even John Clifton, who'd given it his all, hadn't really managed to do that. Somehow, the Cliftons always got by. But a profit?

Not a chance. And for seven years after his dad's tragic death, Grant had tried his damnedest to make a success of the place himself. Same old, same old. Somehow he stayed afloat. Barely. But that was the best he ever did.

It had been the same when Rufus took over. The ranch had yet to go under, but it was no money-maker and Grant didn't believe it ever would be.

He sent Rufus a narrow-eyed look and muttered darkly, "You weren't thrilled in the least when I hired her on to take over for you. And now, all of a sudden, you're her biggest booster?"

Rufus picked up his hat and hit it on his thigh. "It's true. I had my doubts about her runnin' things. But I'm a man who's willing to give credit where credit is due. That girl has got gumption. She's got stamina. She knows what she's doin'. She also has ideas and they are good ones."

"Damn, Rufus. You're starting to scare me. I don't think I've ever seen you so gung ho about anyone—or anything—in all the years you been working here."

Rufus chortled and said something else.

But Grant didn't hear a word of it. He just happened to glance toward the wide-open doors that led to the yard.

He saw Steph.

Steph. In clean Wranglers, fresh boots and a little red shirt that clung to those fine slender curves he'd only that very day realized she had. Her golden hair hung, dry now, sleek and shining as pure silk, to her shoulders.

And those slim hips of hers? They swayed easy.

She tempted him with every step and all she was doing was walking toward him.

Grant watched her coming, struck dumb all over again by how beautiful she was. His breath was all tangled up in his throat and his heart was doing something impossible inside his chest and all of a sudden his jeans were too damn tight.

Damn. He was making a total fool of himself.

All Rufus had to do was look down to see how sweet, innocent, smart-as-a-whip Stephanie affected the boss.

How in the hell, Grant wondered, could this be happening to him?

Chapter Two

Stephanie entered the barn, the bright sun outside lighting her gold hair from behind, creating a halo around her suddenly shadowed face. Grant, his senses spinning, somehow managed to get his boots under him and rise from the bale.

She came right for them. "Hey, you two. Mom said I'd find you out here." She reached him, slid her warm, callused hand into his and flashed him a smile. "C'mon. Got some things I want to show you."

Prickles of awareness seemed to shoot up his arm from the hand she was clutching. Her scent taunted him: shampoo, sunshine and sweetness. It took a serious effort of will not to yank her close and slam his mouth down on hers—with Rufus sitting right there, fingering that cigarette he hadn't quite gotten around to lighting yet.

This is bad. This is...not like me, Grant reminded himself.

And it wasn't. Not like him in the least.

Yeah. All right. He knew that in town, folks considered him something of a ladies' man.

And he did like a pretty woman. What man didn't? But he never obsessed over any of them, never got tongue-tied as a green kid in their presence.

Not until today, anyway.

Stephanie. Of all the women in the world...

By some minor miracle, he found his voice. "Show me what?"

"You'll see." She beamed up at him, those shining eyes green as a matched pair of four-leaf clovers. "Come on." She tugged on his hand.

He let her pull him along, vaguely aware of a chuckle from Rufus behind them and the hissing snap as the cowboy struck a match.

Inside, she led him to the office, which was off the entry hall, not far from the front door. She tugged him over to the desk and pushed him down into the worn leather swivel chair that used to be his dad's.

He sent her a wary glance. "What's this about?"

"You'll see." She turned on the new computer

she'd asked him to buy for her when she started in as top hand.

"What?" he demanded, his senses so full of her, he thought he'd explode.

"Don't be so impatient. Give it a chance to boot up." She leaned over his chair, her gaze on the computer screen, that fragrant hair swinging forward. He watched, transfixed, as she tucked that golden hank of loose hair back behind her ear. He stared at her profile and longed to reach up and run the back of his hand down the smooth golden skin of her throat, to get a fistful of that shining hair and bring it to his mouth so he could feel the silkiness against his lips. "There," she announced. By then, she had her hand on the mouse. She started clicking. "Look at that." She beamed with pride.

He tore his hungry gaze from her face and made himself look at the monitor. "Okay. A spreadsheet."

She laughed. The musical sound seemed to shiver all through him. "Oh, come on. Who's got the fancy business degree from UM? Not me, that's for sure." She pointed. "Look. That's a lot of calves, wouldn't you say? And look at the totals in the yearling column. They're high. I think it's going to be a fine year."

He peered closer at the spreadsheet, frowning. She was right. The yearling count *was* pretty high. He muttered gruffly, "Not bad…"

"I'm working on making sure they're all nice and fat come shipping day. And as far as the calves? I think the total is high there because of that new feed mixture I gave their mamas before calving time. Healthy cows make healthy calves." She laughed again. "Well, duh. As if you didn't know. And you just watch. Next year, when those calves are ready for market, they'll be weighing in at close to seven hundred pounds each—which is really what I'm leading up to here. Yeah, my new feed mixture is looking like a real success. But bottom line? Winter feeding is expensive. Not only because of all the hay we have to put up, but also in the labor-intensive work of caring for and feeding our pregnant cows in the winter months when the feed has got be brought to them. If you really stop and think about it, *we* work for the cows. My idea is to start letting our cows work for us, letting them find their own feed, which they would do, if there was any available during the winter months…"

He watched her mouth move and kept thinking about what it might feel like under his. What it might *taste* like…

She gave him a big smile. "There are changes going on in the industry, Grant. Ranchers are learning that just because a thing has always been done a certain way doesn't automatically mean it's the best, most efficient and profitable way. What I'm getting to here is that lots of ranchers now are switching from spring to summer calving. And you know what?"

He cleared his throat. "Uh. What?"

"It's working for them, Grant. Matching the nutritional needs of the herd to the forage available can cut production costs and improve profitabil…" Her sweet, husky voice trialed off. "Grant? You with me here?"

"Yeah."

"You seem…distracted."

"No. Really. I'm not."

She leaned in a little closer to him, a tiny frown forming between her smooth brows, the amazing scent of her taunting him even more cruelly that a moment before. "Is it…" She spoke so softly, almost shyly, the savvy ranch foreman suddenly replaced by a nervous young girl. "…about earlier?"

He flat out could not think. His mind was one big ball of mush. "Uh. Earlier?"

A flush swept up her satiny throat and stained her cheeks a tempting pink. "Um. You know. At the creek…" Her gold-tipped lashes swept down. And she swore. A very bad word.

It shocked him enough that he let out a laugh. "Steph. Shame on you."

With a low, frustrated sound, she straightened and stepped back. He felt equal parts relief and despair—relief that she was far enough away he wasn't quite so tempted to grab her. Despair that the delicious smell of her no longer swam all around him.

"Damn it," she said—a much milder oath that time. "I am so…dumb. Just…really, completely childish and dumb."

"Uh. Steph."

"What?" She glared at him.

"What are you talking about?"

She flung out a hand. "Oh, please. You know exactly what I'm talking about."

"Er. I do?"

"I keep…beating this silly dead horse to death over and over again. It's just not that huge a deal that you saw me naked, right?" She looked at him pleadingly.

For her sake—and his—he told a whopper of a lie. "No. Not at all. Not a huge deal at all."

"Exactly. It's no big deal and I need to act like a grown-up and let it go. But no. Every time you look at me funny, I'm just sure you're thinking how annoyed or amused or…*whatever* you are at me and it gets me all…flustered and I instantly start babbling away about the whole stupid thing all over again. Oh, I just… Will somebody shoot me? Please. Will somebody just put me clean out of my misery?"

He rose. "Steph."

She put up a hand. "Oh, wait. I know you're going to say something nice. That's how you are. Always so good. So understanding. So…um…" Her eyes widened as he did exactly what he shouldn't do and closed the distance between them. "Wonderful…" she whispered. "Just a wonderful man."

Getting close again was bad enough. But the last thing he ought to do was to put his hands on her. He knew that. He did.

So why the hell was he reaching out and clasping her shoulders?

Damn. Her bones felt so delicate. And the warm silk of her skin where the red shirt ended and her flesh began…

There were no words for that, for the miracle of her skin under his hands. There was nothing.

But the scent of her, the *feel* of her…

She swallowed. "Grant?"

He remembered to speak. "I'm not that wonderful. Take my word for it."

"Oh, Grant…"

"And I want you to know…" The thing was, he could stand here holding her shoulders and looking in her shining eyes for the next decade or so. Just stand here and stare at that dimple in her chin, at her slightly parted lips, her clover-green eyes…

"What?" she asked.

He frowned and, like an idiot, he parroted, "What?"

"You want me to know, what?" Wildly she scanned his face.

And he had no idea what. Not a hint. Not a clue.

And something was happening. Something was changing.

Something about Steph. She was…suddenly different. All at once her nervousness, her girlish embarrassment, had vanished.

Now, he looked down at a woman, a beautiful woman, a woman sure of what she wanted.

"Oh, Grant…" They were the same words she'd said not a minute before.

The same.

And yet totally different.

She lifted her hands and rested them on his chest and before he could remember that he should stop her, she slid them up to encircle his neck.

He shouldn't be doing this, shouldn't be standing here way too close to her, shouldn't be looking down at that mouth of hers, thinking how he'd like nothing better than to cover it with his own.

He shouldn't…

"Oh, Grant. Oh, yeah." And she lifted up on tiptoe and pressed that soft, wide mouth to his.

Chapter Three

Μore things he shouldn't be doing…

He shouldn't be wrapping his arms around her and pulling her close, shouldn't be easing his tongue between those softly parted lips of hers. Shouldn't be sweeping his tongue over the eager surface of hers. Shouldn't be finding the taste of her even sweeter than he'd dared to imagine.

Shouldn't be.

But he was.

He ran an eager hand down the curve of her back and cupped her firm, sleek bottom, pulling her up and into him, nice and tight. So she could feel exactly how she affected him…

Wrong, he thought.

Shouldn't...

But that didn't stop him. He kissed those soft-sighing lips of hers and when she sighed again, he kissed her some more.

She didn't seem to mind.

Far from it. She kissed him right back.

It was good. The best. Better than the best. He didn't want it ever to end.

But he knew that it had to. Exerting a superhuman effort of will, he lifted his mouth from hers.

There was a moment. Breath held. They stared at each other. Her eyes were greener than ever, her lips slightly swollen from that kiss he shouldn't have shared with her.

"I'm sorry," he said, and clasped her shoulders again to put her gently away from him. "I don't know what the hell my problem is. I shouldn't have done that."

And she smiled, a smile that trembled a little at first, and then grew wider. A smile that became so bright, it blinded him. "Oh, yeah," she said. "You should have. And I'm real glad you did."

For the first time ever, Marie's famous pot roast had no taste.

Not to Grant, anyway. The last thing he could think about that evening was food.

In his mind, there was only Steph: her smile, her

laughter, the memory of her kiss, the look in her eyes across the table whenever their glances happened to meet.

He had a really big problem here and he knew it. He kept almost forgetting *who* she was, kept losing sight of the fact that he was sworn to look out for her, that he could never, *ever* hurt her, that the last thing he would ever do was to take her to bed.

He was all wrong for her and he knew it. She was a find-the-right-guy-and-marry-him kind of girl. An innocent in her heart. Hell. He was reasonably sure she was still a virgin.

A virgin. Oh God.

Grant didn't go out with virgins.

And wasn't up for the whole marriage-and-family deal. Not now. Not ever.

And even if she didn't expect him to marry her, a girl like Steph would at least want something approximating what women liked to call a *relationship*. Grant didn't have *relationships*.

When it came to women, he liked things free and easy, fun and open-ended.

And sitting at the dinner table that evening, he felt trapped. Boxed in by his own burning lust for sweet little Stephanie Julen.

He needed to stay away from her. Oh, yeah. Since he couldn't keep his hands off her once he got close, the solution was simple: He would keep his distance. Yeah. That should work. If he just stayed away…

He poked more food he didn't taste into his mouth and resolutely chewed.

Marie asked, "Grant, are you feeling all right?"

He swallowed. Hard. "Uh, yeah. I'm just fine."

"You're looking a little strange. Is the pot roast okay?"

"The best. As always."

Rufus let loose with one of those low, knowing chortles of his. Grant sent him a dark look.

The old cowboy shrugged. "Hell, Marie. This is the best you ever made. Nothin' wrong with this here pot roast, nosirree. It's tender and juicy. Perfect in every way. Just like the potatoes and the carrots and these rolls of yours that are fluffy as little pillows. Uh-uh. If the boss has got a problem, it's not with the food." He forked up a big bite and stuffed it into his mouth.

"I don't know what you're talking about, old man. I've got no problem at all." Grant scowled at Rufus for all he was worth.

"Hear that?" Rufus grinned good and wide. "Boss says he ain't got a problem." He raised his beer. "I'll drink to that."

Grant looked away from the old man—and saw that Jim, the new hand, was staring at Steph. Grant resisted the urge to tell the fool to get his eyes back in his head where they belonged.

After all, who was he to tell Jim not to look at Steph? The cowhand seemed like a nice enough guy. Steph had mentioned after she hired him that he was a good worker. Rufus said he kept his area of the bunkhouse clean and in order. Maybe Jim was hoping to settle down, find himself a suitable woman and ask her to be his wife. If so, he'd be a lot better match for Steph than Grant ever would.

But Steph wasn't looking at the hired hand. Steph was looking at *him*. And every time she looked at him, he wanted to jump up and grab her and carry her off someplace nice and private, someplace where he could peel off that red shirt and those snug jeans and have another long look at what he'd seen down by the creek.

He covered pretty well, he thought. Except for Rufus's sly remarks and the occasional shining glance from Steph, they all kind of carried on as usual.

There was pie and ice cream after the meal. Grant dutifully packed it away. And then, at last, Marie started clearing off.

"It was great, Marie. Thanks." He slid his napkin in at the side of his plate and pushed back his chair. "And it's an hour's ride back to the resort. I think I'd better get moving."

Rufus grunted. "Your horse is ready to go. Tacked him up before I came in to eat."

"'Preciate that." He pushed his chair under the table, and turned for the entry hall. The hat he'd borrowed waited on the peg by the front door. He grabbed it, yanked the door back and fled.

Too bad Steph was right behind him.

She caught up with him out on the porch. He didn't know what the hell to say to her. So he said nothing. She didn't seem to mind, just strolled along at his side across the yard to the post beside the barn where Rufus had hitched Titan.

As they reached the big gelding, she spoke. "Nice out now. Cooling off a little…"

The sun was just sliding behind the mountains, but it would be a while yet till dark. "Yeah," he said, without actually looking at her. "Nice." He took the reins and mounted. Then he made the mistake of glancing down at her.

She smiled. That wide, glowing, happy smile. Something tightened in his chest.

"How about a picnic?" she asked. "I can't tomorrow. We've got too many fences that need fixing around here—not to mention a couple of ditches that have to be burned out so those fat yearlings I've been bragging on won't die of thirst. But I could get away Tuesday. Say, noon? I'll meet you out by that big, dead cottonwood over in the Danvers pasture." He'd ridden by that tree earlier on his way to the ranch. Once, it had been on Triple J land. She asked, "You know where I mean?"

Tell her how you just can't make it. "Yeah. I know."

"It's about midway between here and the resort, so it won't take you all that long to get there. Over the fence from that pasture is Parks Service land

and some nice shade trees. I'll bring the blanket and Mom's cold chicken. And the beer."

Tell her no, you can't make it. Tell her it's just not possible. Tell her now.

"All right. Noon on Tuesday," he heard himself say.

"Good night, Grant." She stepped back.

He tipped his hat and turned his horse to go.

The whole ride back, he called himself a hundred kinds of damn fool. Now, he'd have to call her. Tell her how something had come up and he just couldn't make it on Tuesday, no way.

He was so busy stewing over how he shouldn't have kissed her, shouldn't have agreed to any damn picnic, that he didn't even think about what he'd forgotten to do until he was back in his suite at the resort, changing his clothes. He stopped with one leg out of his Wranglers and gaped at his image in the wall-to-wall mirror of his dressing area.

He'd never told them he was selling the ranch.

"Mom?" Steph leaned in the archway from the front hall.

Marie looked up from her mending and smiled a tired smile. She took off the dimestore glasses she wore for close work and rubbed the bridge of her nose. In the pool of light cast by the lamp, her round face looked shadowed and lined, older than her forty-nine years. "Off to bed?"

"Mmm-hmm." It wasn't quite nine yet, but

Steph—and her mother, too—would be up and working long before first light. "Just wanted to say good-night."

Marie set her mending in her lap and reached to pat the arm of the sofa a few feet from her favorite chair. "Sit a minute."

Something in her mother's tone alerted Steph. "What's wrong?"

"Come on. Just sit with me. Not for long…"

Reluctantly, sensing she wasn't going to like what her mother had to say, Steph left the archway. She took the spot at the end of the sofa. "What is it?"

Suddenly Marie just had to take a couple more stitches in the sock she was mending. Steph stared at her bent head, feeling fondness mixed with apprehension. She loved and respected her mother. Most of the time, the two of them saw eye to eye.

But tonight, Steph had a feeling they were about to disagree.

At last, Marie looked up again. "You and Grant got something going on between you?"

Steph couldn't hide her trembling smile. "Oh, I hope so."

Marie stitched some more. Then, abruptly, she lowered her work to her lap again. "He's far from ready to settle down."

"I know, Mom."

"You two want different things from life."

"True. But…you never know how things might turn out."

Her mother shook her head. "You should see yourself. Pink cheeks and stars in your eyes…"

"Is that so bad?"

"You watch your heart, honey."

"Oh, Mom. There's nothing to watch. My heart belongs to him and it always has."

Grant had meetings all day Monday. From concierge to housekeeping to the AspenGlow Spa to food service to sales to public relations—and more—Grant was responsible for overseeing it all.

The longest meeting was first thing. From nine until eleven-thirty, he pored over plans for the projected 18-hole, par seventy-two championship golf course, which was still in the early stages of development, with construction scheduled to begin next summer.

At eleven forty-five, he met with his assistant to go over the calendar for the week. After that, he *could* have stolen a few minutes to call the ranch and tell them about the sale.

But no. It really wasn't the kind of news he wanted to deliver in a phone call. He felt he owed it to the hands and Steph and her mom to give it to them face-to-face. And there was just no opportunity for that, not that day.

True, he had no appointments that evening. He

could make the time to drive out there after six. And maybe he should...

But the more he thought about it, the more it seemed best to clear his calendar for a few hours Tuesday afternoon and meet Steph for that picnic as planned. He could tell her then. And after he told her, he could ride back to the ranch with her and share the news with the rest of them.

In the meantime, he needed to prove to himself that what had happened the day before was not going to happen again. He needed to be sure that yesterday was just...some kind of fluke. A strange, over-the-top reaction to seeing Steph naked down by the creek, an offshoot of the sudden realization that she wasn't a kid anymore.

Now that he had some distance from the situation, he knew there was really nothing to worry about. Steph might be all grown-up, but she was still like a sister to him. A sister. Nothing more.

And there were a whole lot of pretty women in the world. A nice romantic evening with a fun, friendly gorgeous female would do the trick, put things firmly back into perspective for him.

As luck would have it, just such a woman called while he was in the first of his afternoon meetings. She left him a message in voice mail. She lived in San Diego and had come for the skiing in January when they'd hooked up. He'd enjoyed every moment he'd spent with her.

"I had such a great time last winter," her recorded voice teased, "I decided to try my luck over the Fourth. I'm up in the Thunder Ridge condos with a girlfriend. Give me a buzz when you get in. I can't wait to see you. *All* of you…"

He returned her call and set up a date for that night. His receptionist beeped him just as he was saying goodbye.

He hung up and punched the other line. "What?"

"Eva Post's on two."

Eva was his realtor. "Eva. Hey."

"Grant. I've got the offer. It's exactly as promised. The acceptance deadline is tomorrow at five, so we need to get together. We'll go over all the points in detail, as a matter of course, before you sign. But I guarantee you're going to be very happy. They're giving you everything you asked for."

"What about the closing date?"

"September first. The buyer was hoping we could make it sooner, but I explained that you needed time to shut your operation down."

"September first…" It was a reasonable date and he knew it. But still, it seemed like no time at all.

"No worries, I promise," Eva coaxed. "It's in the contract that you can take whatever time you need over the next *six* months to sell off the stock and equipment. As long as the main house, the bunkhouse and the foreman's cottage are ready for the buyer to move in by nine-one, she's happy."

She was Melanie McFarlane, an Easterner who'd shown up in town a few weeks ago and was staying in the main lodge at the resort. Melanie came from money. She had a degree in hotel management and she was buying Clifton's Pride as an "investment," she said. She planned to make the place into a guest ranch.

Grant's father would never have allowed such a thing. But John Clifton was dead. The price was more than right and Melanie's financing was rock-solid.

The only problem: Grant's concern for his people. Damn it, he should have carried through yesterday as planned, not let himself get sidetracked by the new, grown-up Steph. It was plain wrong for him to sell Clifton's Pride out from under them before he'd even *told* them he was doing it. And as things stood now, he wouldn't be telling them until tomorrow afternoon.

Eva asked, "How about four o'clock? You can come out to my office, or I can come to you."

"Four o'clock...today?"

"Not working for you?"

"How about tomorrow? Late afternoon. Say, four-thirty?"

"That's cutting it right down to the wire," the realtor warned. He said nothing. After a moment, she let it go. "My office?" she suggested.

"No. Mine."

The realtor agreed and said goodbye.

It would work out fine, Grant promised himself.

He'd tell Steph and the others the news tomorrow—
and return to the office to sign the papers afterward.

Grant's date sent him a sultry look from under
her thick black lashes. They stood at the door to her
friend's condo. From her expression, he had a pretty
good idea what was coming next.

And it was.

"My roommate's away for the night," she said.
"Come in for a drink? Just so happens I've got a
magnum of Cristal chilling." He saw her expectations
in her dark eyes. They'd had one fine time last January.
Lots of laughs and some good, hot sex. She had every
reason to assume it would be the same tonight.

He'd *planned* for it to be the same tonight.

But since yesterday, nothing seemed to be going
as he planned.

Through drinks in the resort's lounge and dinner
in the Gallatin Room, he kept wondering what the
hell he was doing there. Wondering made him distracted and that caused long, awkward lags in the
conversation. She'd asked him three or four times
if he was all right.

He'd sworn he was fine, but they both knew the
night was one big loser. Surprising, now he thought
about it, that she'd even bothered to invite him in.
He wished she hadn't—not now that he realized he
just couldn't give her what she wanted from him.

So much for putting things back in perspective with the help of a fun, friendly, gorgeous gal.

"Thanks," he said. "But I've got an early meeting tomorrow."

She blinked. But she recovered quickly. He knew what she was thinking: If he was fool enough to turn her down, it was *his* loss. She moved close and he got a whiff of her perfume. Musky. Exotic. A scent he'd found damn sexy last winter.

Hell. He still found it sexy. Just...not for him.

She touched his cheek, her hand smooth and cool. He thought of Steph's hand—sun-warmed, rough with calluses—and it hit him like a mule kick to the gut.

All his denials meant exactly nothing.

He wanted Steph so bad, it was causing him to do the strangest things—like forgetting to tell her he was selling the ranch she loved so damn much. Like turning down a hot night with a fine, sexy woman, an experienced woman who knew a lot of really impressive, inventive ways to please a man...

He was in big trouble and he didn't know what to do about it.

"'Night, then," his date said, and went in.

He returned to his offices in the resort's corporate headquarters down the hill from main lodge. There was always plenty of work to catch up on and he didn't feel a whole lot like sleeping anyway.

* * *

By the next morning, Grant had himself convinced all over again that he really had no problem when it came to Stephanie. No problem at all.

He would meet her at noon, as agreed. He'd feel what he'd always felt toward her before Sunday: fondness and protectiveness—along with some serious apprehension, which was only natural since she was bound to be upset when she learned about the sale of Clifton's Pride.

Riley Douglas, who was technically comanager of the resort, but who had a lot of irons in the fire and pretty much left the job to Grant, came by at nine. Grant brought him up to speed on the progress with the golf course. Then they discussed the pros and cons of opening a third full-service restaurant at the main lodge. They already had the upscale Gallatin Room and the Grubstake, where you could get a great burger and all-day breakfast. Grant thought they needed something in the middle range.

Riley agreed. "Come up with a few specifics— like who, what, how and how much. Then we'll bring it before the board."

Grant asked after Caleb, Riley's dad. The resort had been Caleb's brainchild. The wealthy rancher had provided the land, put together the investor group and overseen the original project's development. Without the drive and influence of Caleb Douglas, the resort wouldn't exist—let alone been a raging success from the day it opened for business last November.

Riley shook his head. "Sad to say my dad is gettin' old, slowing down a little…"

"Give him my best, will you—and your mom, too?"

Riley promised that he would.

After Riley took off, there were a couple of food service issues to settle and some calls to return. Grant had the decks more or less cleared by eleven and at eleven-twenty he was mounted on Titan and headed for the Danvers pasture.

Once he left the stable yard behind, he urged the horse to a gallop, all too aware of a certain rising feeling in his chest, an eagerness in his blood.

Steph was there, waiting on Trixiebelle, beside the twisted old cottonwood in the pasture that had once been part of her father's land. He saw her and his heart started pounding hard and deep and needful. Heat streaked through him, searing as it went.

Trixiebelle danced to the side as he rode up. With a horsewoman's sure skill, Steph calmed the mare. Her strong, capable hand on the horse's neck, she beamed him a wide, happy smile—a smile that made his head spin and his blood race even faster through his veins.

Damn. She was beautiful. So beautiful, it hurt. Her hat hung down her back and her hair, pulled loosely into a single braid, caught the sun in golden gleams. And those eyes…

Green as spring grass.

"Come on," she said, and pointed to a stand of birch trees maybe a quarter of a mile away. "Over there." She turned the horse and took off.

Hopelessly ensnared, forgetting everything but the color of her eyes and the way her hair shone like a handful of nuggets in the sunlight, he followed.

Chapter Four

Steph spread the blanket in the dappled shade of the trees.

She had plans for today. Big ones. Romantic ones. Plans that involved slow, lazy kisses and tender, arousing caresses.

And, just maybe, even more.

Funny, but she wasn't the least bit nervous. She *was* excited. Kind of tingly all over. Her heart felt full to bursting.

At last. After all these years of loving Grant Clifton and knowing his feelings for her were strictly the brotherly kind, she saw her chance with him.

And she was taking that chance, going all the

way with it. No matter what anyone thought. No matter what her mother said.

"Here we go." He was back with the rocks she'd sent him to find. He knelt and placed four nice, big flat ones, each on a corner of the blanket to hold it in place against the ever-present wind.

"Great." She sent him a glance that lingered a little too long. Heat arced between them. He was the one who looked away, rising again and stepping back.

Oh, yes. She was certain. He wanted her and she did have a chance with him.

No, she wasn't quite so naive as her mom seemed to think. She didn't imagine that Grant loved her. Uh-uh. He did not. And as dewy-eyed as she was feeling, she intended to remember that. He thought she was innocent. But she wasn't—not in her heart. Not in her tough and pragmatic rancher's mind.

Stephanie Julen was a realist and she knew what Grant felt for her: He wanted her. A lot. He wanted her—and he didn't *want* to want her. He'd always considered it his job to protect her.

And now he intended to protect her from himself.

She was a whole lot more woman than he realized, however. And as a woman, she would do all in her power to see that he put those noble intentions aside and got what he wanted. After all, it was only what *she* wanted, too.

It had taken her a while to catch on, painful hours

on Sunday—between the time he found her at the creek and the kiss they shared in the office. She'd been so sure he was mad at her or shocked or disgusted or something else equally upsetting.

But eventually, she'd figured it out. That strange look in his eyes every time he glanced her way… why, it was a *hungry* look.

And if she'd had a single doubt that he desired her, the kiss had burned all uncertainty clean away.

Oh, that kiss. He'd kissed her as if he wanted to gobble her right up.

And, well, Steph wouldn't mind at all being gobbled. Not as long as it was Grant doing the gobbling. Oh, my, yes. She got chills all through her every time she thought about that kiss, about the hard, strong feel of his body pressed close to hers, about the way he'd swept his big hand down and cupped her bottom and pressed her closer still.

She'd felt what she did to him then, oh, yes, she had. She'd felt what he wanted to do to *her.* She'd felt it and known that she was getting her chance with him. At last.

No regrets, she promised herself. She would take things with Grant as they came. Ride this wild horse and just hope against hope that maybe she'd manage to stay on.

He was a good man. And a generous one. A protector of the weak and the needy. A man you could count on when you were down.

But he was not looking for a wife. What did he need with a lifetime commitment, or even a steady girl? The women flocked to him and he seemed to thoroughly enjoy his bachelor lifestyle.

Stephanie really hoped she could make him see that even a man who had everything needed the right woman to stand by his side. But she wasn't counting on anything. She had no expectations of how it would all work out.

He stood back, watching from under the brim of his hat, as she went to where they'd hobbled the horses and began taking their lunch from the insulated saddlebags. She glanced over her shoulder, sent him another smile and thrilled to the lovely flare of heat that sparked in his eyes.

"I couldn't resist the urge to race you over here," she said. "And that means the beer is nothing but foam about now. You'll have to wait for it."

"It's fine," he said, his voice low and a little bit ragged.

"I've got lemonade, though."

"I love lemonade."

She laughed. "No, you don't. But until the beer settles, lemonade is what you're getting." She unloaded the plastic jar of lemonade, the food and the forks and paper goods, taking way too much pleasure out of knowing that he watched every move she made—hungrily, like some big mountain lion stretched out on a tree limb, his tail flicking lazily, eyeing his dinner. She loved knowing it wasn't just her mom's cold chicken he was hungry for.

Once she had all the food out, she dropped to the blanket and took off her boots.

"What are you doing?" he growled.

She had to cover a laugh. For a ladies' man, he sure was acting edgy and nervous today. She wiggled her stocking foot at him and answered in an easy tone. "Just getting comfortable." She set her boots in the grass, tucked her legs to the side and patted the empty space next to her. "Come on. Let's eat."

He approached with caution and again, she had to hide a smile. But when he reached her, he turned, dropped to the edge of the blanket—and took off his own boots. She watched the muscles in his back bunch and stretch beneath the worn fabric of his old Western shirt and felt a heat down low in her belly, a sort of melting, lazy sensation. She wanted…

His mouth on hers. His knowing hands stroking her body.

Whoa, girl. Slow down a little. All in good time.

He set the boots away from the blanket, set his hat on them and faced her, drawing his long legs up, sitting cross-legged. She served him: a paper cup of lemonade, a breast and a drumstick, a mound of potato salad, a buttered roll and some carrot sticks. Over the years, she'd watched him eat hundreds of times. She knew how much food he liked, what parts of the chicken he preferred.

"It's good," he said, as he dug in.

She was filling her own plate from the plastic containers. "Oh, yeah." She tasted the potato salad. "Mmm. My mom. She sure can cook."

He waved the drumstick at her. "You mean you didn't fry this chicken yourself?"

She laughed, glad that he seemed to be relaxing a little. "Don't worry. I wouldn't do that to you." She knew how to cook. Marie had insisted on teaching her the basics, at least. But she was always much too impatient to hang around the kitchen. She wanted to be out the door and on the back of a horse. So her biscuits ended up gooey in the center and half the time her chicken got charred. "I know my limitations. I'm a rancher, not a ranch wife."

He set the chicken leg back on his plate. Suddenly he seemed kind of thoughtful. "You're happy, huh? Working cattle? Up before dawn to get the chores done, freezing your butt off all winter, dripping sweat while you fix fences and burn out ditches in the blazing summer sun?"

She tipped her head to the side and studied his face. "What kind of question is that? You know me. Does a dog have fleas? Do bats fly?"

He frowned. But when he spoke, his voice

sounded offhand. "Just making sure you remember there are other options for you."

"Too bad there's nothing else I want to do."

"But there are other things you *could* do. As I recall, you got As and Bs in high school."

"I'll have you know I got straight As."

"I'm impressed."

"I did my best in school. That doesn't mean I enjoyed being there." She wouldn't have gone past the eighth grade if her mom and Grant hadn't insisted she get her diploma. And she still believed she could have held on to the Triple J, if only she'd been able to work full-time, instead of spending five days out of seven at Thunder Canyon High.

He advised in a weary tone, "You scrunch up your face like that, it might get stuck."

"Hah," she said. "You sound like Mom."

He chuckled. "Just don't be bitter. Believe me, it was the best thing. You'd have regretted not finishing high school."

"No. I wouldn't have. But it's okay—and I'm *not* bitter." She wrinkled her nose at him again. "Well, not much, anyway…"

He ate half of his flaky, perfect dinner roll. She chomped a carrot stick and got to work on a tender, crispy-skinned thigh. Eventually he said, "What I was trying to tell you is that I'm doin' pretty well now. I could help you out, if you decided you might want to give college a try…"

Emotion tightened her throat. Not because she felt she'd missed out on college, not because she wanted it. She didn't. Not in the least.

It was just that he was always so good to her, so generous. "Oh, Grant. Thank you. But no. I'm pretty much a self-starter. If I need to know something, I find a way to learn it. I never had a yen for any formal higher education. All I've ever wanted was a chance to do exactly what I'm doing now."

"I see." His voice was flat. He set his plate down beside him, only half-finished.

Distress made a leaden sensation in her stomach. "Okay. I don't get it. What did I say?"

He stared at her for a long, strange moment. And then he shrugged and picked up his plate again. "It's nothing."

"Are you sure?"

"Absolutely."

"But you—"

"No buts, Steph. I am positive to the millionth degree." He grinned as he said it.

She grunted. "Oh, very funny."

The Christmas she was seven, five years before their dads were killed, her mom had tried to talk her into asking Santa for one of those fancy American Girl dolls, the kind that came with a whole perfect miniature wardrobe—and a doll-size trunk to put all those fine clothes in.

Steph had sworn that a doll was the last thing she

needed. She wanted a pony more than anything. She knew she was old enough for a horse of her own.

Grant, a high-school senior that year, had been over at the house, for some reason long lost to her now. She'd been following her mom around the kitchen, arguing endlessly, "I mean it, Mama. Don't you get me any doll. I don't want a doll and if you get me one I'll rip its head off. I need my own horse. I got work to do. Just ask Daddy. He'll tell you I'm his best helper and his best helper needs a horse."

Grant had stuck his head in from the living room to tease, "Oh, come on, Steffie, you know you want a pretty little doll."

She still remembered whipping around to glare at him, shaking a finger as she lectured him, "Do not call me Steffie. And I don't want any doll."

"You sure?"

"I am positive, Grant Clifton," she'd smartly informed him. "Positive to the millionth degree."

Now, he lifted his drumstick to her in a salute. "You were one feisty kid."

She faked a groan. "Oh, please. Feisty? Not me. I was a *practical* kid. And I got my first horse that Christmas, if you recall."

Malomar, her sweet-natured bay mare, had ended up sold at auction with the rest of the Triple J stock. It was one of her saddest memories: her mare being led into that horse trailer, the trailer kicking up dust as it rolled away.

That memory, somehow, was almost as bad as seeing her dad's lifeless body with that big red hole in the side of his head on the day that he died. The death of a parent was an enormous and terrible thing—too terrible in some ways for a young mind to comprehend. But the end of her life as she'd known and loved it?

That had been horrible, too. And by then, three years after her dad died, she'd been old enough to understand what was happening when she watched Malomar being taken away.

But she wasn't dwelling on any sad memories today. Uh-uh. She had the man she loved sitting right beside her, and he was finally seeing her as a woman grown. She fully intended to enjoy every minute of this afternoon.

They ate in silence for a little while, finishing off their drumsticks and potato salad, sipping their lemonade.

Finally Grant said, "I remember that you got your horse that Christmas, just like you wanted—and promptly fell off her and broke your collarbone."

She confessed, "It's true. I was never what you'd call a cautious kid."

"Uh-uh. You were brave and bold and nobody ever told you what to do." Those sky-blue eyes of his gleamed at her. She saw admiration in them.

For the fearless kid she'd once been? Or the woman she was now?

Or maybe…both? Her heart skipped a beat at the thought.

And then he was frowning again. "Look. Steph. There's something I really have to—"

"Oh, don't," she cried before he could finish.

Now he seemed puzzled. "Don't?"

"That's right. Don't. I know just what you're going to say and I don't want to hear it, okay?"

He actually gulped. "Er, you *know?*"

She set her plate aside and wiped her hands on a paper towel. "Of course, I know. How could I not? Something like this, a woman always knows. I admit, you had me wondering at first. But I got the message eventually. Really, it's all just so…perfectly obvious."

"Obvious." He gaped at her.

"Yes."

He set his own plate down. And he knocked back the rest of his lemonade, crushing the paper cup in his big fist when he finished. And he swore under his breath. "Steph."

"Yeah?"

"What, exactly, are you talking about?"

Should she say it right out? Probably not. Her mom always used to tell her that men didn't like it when a woman got too direct, when a woman dared to take the lead in an obvious way.

But her mom was from a different generation,

after all. From a time when women were expected to wait around for men to make the first move.

Thank God it wasn't like that anymore.

But still, what if she spooked him by laying it right out there, bold as you please? She didn't want to scare him off.

A sudden gust of wind stirred the trees around them and tried to blow the paper plates away, with only chicken bones to hold them down.

"Oops." Swiftly she gathered up the remains of their meal, stuffed it in the trash bag she'd brought and weighted the bag down with a rock. "There," she said unnecessarily when that job was done. He was sitting so still, watching her, kind of narrow-eyed, waiting for her to explain herself.

She stalled some more. "Hey. Want a beer?" She started to rise.

"Stay here." He reached for his boots. "I can get it." He pulled on his boots and grabbed the trash bag from under the rock. "You want one?"

She didn't much care for beer. "No."

She watched him go to the horses, something inside her kind of aching in a joyous way. His shoulders were so broad, his waist so hard and narrow. And he truly did have one fine butt.

And how could she tell him—that she knew he wanted her though he didn't *want* to want her? How could she make him understand that she didn't expect anything from him?

Except maybe his kisses and his eager embrace. Just this...wonder. And this joy.

And as for the rest? Well, why not just let the rest take care of itself?

He stuffed the trash in the saddlebags, got a beer and returned to her. She stewed some more over what to say to him as he set the can on one of the rocks and pulled off his boots all over again. He popped the tab and took a long drink. She watched his Adam's apple bounce up and down and continued her internal debate: What to say?

How to say it?

Finally he set down what was left of the beer. "Well?"

"Um. Yeah. Okay. I..." The words were right there, inside her mind, so clear. *I know that you're attracted to me, but you're thinking it's not right because you're not looking for anything permanent. You're telling yourself you won't take advantage of me. But oh, please. Take advantage. Take advantage right now....*

So clear. And so much easier to *think* than to actually say.

"What?" His gaze locked on hers. "Say it."

"It's...a beautiful day, don't you think?" Oh, Lord. How lame could she get?

"Steph..." His eyes said he couldn't make up his mind between reaching out and grabbing her—or jumping up and running clean away from her as fast as he could go.

"A beautiful day…" She said those lame words again and that time, she swayed toward him. He stiffened. She landed against his chest and looked up at him longingly. "And it's just you and me, all alone on this blanket under the trees…" She put her hand over his heart. Oh, it felt so good. So perfect, just leaning against him. Her breath was all knotted up in her throat. She wanted to stay right where she was, forever, yet she was absolutely certain that any second now, he would push her away.

But he didn't. With a low groan, he gathered her close. "Damn it, Steph."

She laid a finger against his wonderful mouth. "Shh. Okay? Just…shh."

He stared down at her. She could feel the warmth and the strength of him, the shape of him, so hard and manly. And cradled close against him like this, she could feel his heart, too, beating away in there, firm and deep. He said gruffly, "I can't…think, when I touch you."

"Good," she told him, feeling braver now, her love and her yearning leading her on. "Because you don't need to think. I don't *want* you to think."

His lip twitched. It was almost a smile. "Always so damn sure of yourself."

"Oh, no," she cried. "I'm not sure of myself at all. But I am sure about how I feel. Sure about… what I want."

"This is crazy." But his arms tightened around her.

"Oh, no. Not crazy. Right. Exactly right."

"You smell like sunshine," he whispered, the sound rough, as if it hurt him, just to get those words out. "And the way you feel, in my arms, when I touch you…"

"Just kiss me," she whispered back, lifting her mouth to him. "Just kiss me and the rest will take care of itself."

"Shouldn't…" The single word came out on another groan.

"Oh, yes. You should…" So…heady. This magic. This power she was finding she had over him. The magic of wanting. The power of desire.

Who knew it could be like this between a man and woman? She never would have guessed. Every nerve in her body seemed to be singing. She was shivery—but with wonderful, heavy, lazy heat.

"Damn. You're killing me, you know that?"

"Oh, Grant…"

He took her by the arms then, and she was sure all over again that he would set her away from him.

But in the end, he only grabbed her closer as his warm mouth swooped down and covered hers.

Oh, it was amazing. Her senses swam at the feel of him, pressing her close, his hands stroking her back as his tongue traced the seam where her lips met. With a sigh, she let them part for him.

He speared his tongue inside. She sucked on it, boldly, and when he retreated, she followed him, into the warm, hot cave beyond those wonderful lips of his.

She clutched his shoulders as he guided her down onto the blanket. He kissed her more deeply, still, his tongue delving in, sweeping along the edges of her teeth, stroking her own tongue in a long, wet glide.

Oh, it was heaven.

Just as she'd dreamed it might be.

His hand cupped her breast. Beneath her shirt and bra, her nipple hardened, aching. She moaned and lifted her body toward him, wanting more.

Wanting everything. Ready to have it all, at last, right there, on that blanket, in the lovely, shadowed, private place beneath the birch trees…

To have it all with Grant, as she'd always dreamed. To be fully a woman at last, with the only man she'd ever loved.

He kissed her chin, nipping it, whispering her name against her eager flesh. He kissed the side of her neck, opening his mouth there, licking her skin, making her shiver in the most delicious way…

He kissed the hollow of her throat and she stretched her neck back, spearing her fingers into his hair, cupping his head and cradling him close, urging him to kiss her some more, to keep on kissing her.

To never stop.

"Oh, Grant," she whispered, "Oh, Grant. Yes. Please. Yes…"

His warm hand trailed downward. She wanted…more.

To be closer, to have his hand *there,* where she was aching and yearning, hot and eager. To have *him,* completely. To *be* with him in the most passionate, intimate way.

She moaned his name again.

And then, out of nowhere, for no reason at all…he tore himself away from her. With a low groan, and a guttural, "No!" he was gone.

"Grant?" She opened her eyes to see him sitting back on his bent legs, his strong hands on his knees, face flushed, mouth swollen, eyes heavy with the same need that made her legs and arms feel weighted, that made her body so lazy and hungry and hot. She lifted yearning arms to him. "Come back here. Back here to me…"

He swore. "No. This is all wrong. I didn't come here for this."

"But I don't…"

"Damn it, Steph. Listen. Listen to me."

Stunned, punch-drunk with longing, she dragged herself to a sitting position. "I don't understand. What's the matter? What happened?"

He rocked back on his stocking feet and rose above her. She stared up at him, so tall and strong, glaring down at her, the leaves of the birches rustling above his head, the blue, clear sky beyond…

A sudden chill swept through her. She wrapped her arms around herself against a cold that came from deep inside. "What? Say it. Whatever it is, just please, say it. Now."

And at last, he did. "I came out here to tell you I'm selling Clifton's Pride."

Chapter Five

Grant stared down into her flushed, bewildered face. Right then, there were no words to describe how thoroughly he despised himself. As he watched, the hectic color drained from her cheeks and her mouth formed a round, shocked O.

On a husk of breath, she pleaded, "No..."

He forced a nod. "Yeah. It's true. I'm selling the ranch."

She gaped some more, then whispered, "When?"

"I'm signing the contract today, at four-thirty."

She swallowed, caught her upper lip between her teeth, worried it, let it go. "Today."

"That's right."

"When…do we have to be out?"

"By the end of August. The new owner wants to take possession September first."

She seemed to consider that for a moment. "Not quite two months, then… Who?"

"What?"

"Who will be the new owner?"

"Her name's Melanie McFarlane. From out of town. She wants to make it a guest ranch."

"A guest ranch," she repeated as if the very words made her sick.

Grant felt like something squirming and loathsome, something you'd find buried in sour soil under a giant rock. He made himself confess the rest. "I meant to tell you Sunday," he said, as if that mattered. As if that made any difference at all.

"Oh," she said. "You meant to tell us. But you… forgot?"

"I was…distracted."

Color stained her cheeks again and he knew that *she* knew why he hadn't. Because he'd seen her down by the creek, seen her as a woman for the first time. Because his senses, his mind, all of him, had been filled with her. No room left to remember what he *should* have done.

She hitched in a hard breath. "Distracted. By me?"

"Yeah."

"And again, today, right? It's all my fault…"

"I didn't say that. Of course, it's not your fault."

"You met me here to tell me you were selling the ranch. And I *distracted* you again."

"No. Wait. You're getting it all wrong. There's no excuse for my not telling you. I know there's not. I'm not blaming you."

She only stared at him. And he saw it all, his own complete culpability, right there in her upturned face, in those amazing leaf-green eyes of hers: the kiss on Sunday. And worse than that, what he'd almost done just now, out in the open beneath birches, where anyone might ride by and see them. He'd been too busy kissing her to tell her the thing she most needed to know, too absorbed in the feel and the taste of her, too stupefied by his own lust for her, to be straight with her.

His throat felt like two angry hands were squeezing it. Still, roughly, he made himself say the things he'd planned to say before he made such a complete mockery of her innocent trust in him. "It's time to move on. To let go of the past. The world is changing, Steph. The day of the small, family ranch is over. Thunder Canyon isn't the sleepy mountain town it once was. Growth and change are inevitable and we all need to get with the program, we need to—"

She put up a hand. "Wait."

"Uh. What?"

"Don't give me a load of that *progress* crap, please. The last couple of years, it's about *all* I've heard. I don't need to hear anymore. Bottom line is you're selling Clifton's Pride. I get it. It's your ranch, after all, and your choice to make. You can let that buyer of yours turn a fine working ranch into some silly showplace where city people can play at being cowboys if you want to."

He winced. "Look. What matters is, you're going to be okay. I'll see to it, I swear to you, we'll get you a good job. Your mom, too…and I meant what I said about college. If you think you might change your mind, now you'll be leaving the ranch, I'll be glad to foot the bill…"

She just sat there, staring up at him. It was damned unnerving. He couldn't tell what she might be thinking—he only knew it wasn't good.

After the silence stretched out for way too long, she finally asked, "Well. Are you done?"

"I…" Hell. What more was there to say? "Yeah. I'm done."

"Great." She grabbed her boots from the edge of the blanket and yanked them on. Then she settled her hat on her head, gathered her legs under her and stood.

"Put your boots on," she said in a voice so controlled it made him want to grab her and shake her and beg her to yell at him, to go ahead and get it out, tell him exactly what she thought of him. After all, it couldn't be worse than what he thought of himself.

But he didn't grab her. He knew if he did, he'd only try to kiss her again.

God. He was low. *Lower* than low.

He sat, put his hat on and then his boots.

She asked in a tone that was heartbreakingly civil, "Now, would you please get off the blanket so I can roll it up?"

He glanced at his Rolex. There was time—to ride to the ranch, say what needed saying—and get back to his office by four-thirty to meet Eva. He grabbed his beer and gulped the rest of it down, then shook out the can and crushed it.

She took it from him and put it in her saddlebags. He rolled the blanket. She took that from him, too, and tied it behind her saddle.

They mounted up.

"See you tomorrow," she said, her clean-scrubbed, beautiful face absolutely expressionless.

"Uh. Tomorrow?"

She looked at him as if she wondered where he'd put his brains. "It's the Fourth, remember? The parade?"

That's right. Every year, the town put on an Independence Day parade. They'd both agreed to ride the resort's float. Terrific. Another opportunity for her to treat him like the pond scum he was. "Of course, I remember."

Something flashed in her eyes. He couldn't read the emotion. Anger? Hurt? Some bleak combination of both? He didn't know.

He felt like a stranger, an interloper, someone

evil and cruel. And still, even now, when she looked at him as if she didn't know him, didn't *want* to know him, *he* only wanted to drag her right off that mare of hers and into his hungry arms. He wanted to touch her all over, to take off her shirt and her jeans and her boots, to strip her naked and finish what they'd started a little while ago.

She tightened her knees on Trixiebelle and off she went. Grant shook himself and urged Titan to follow.

Steph reined in and leveled a far too patient look at him. "In case you've forgotten, the resort's that way."

"I'm going with you."

She blew out a hard breath. "Haven't you done enough?"

"I have to tell them."

"No, you don't. I'll do it."

"No. That wouldn't be right."

Her glance slid away. He knew what she was thinking—after the way he'd behaved, he had no place talking about what was right. But in the end, she only said, "Suit yourself," and clicked her tongue for Trixiebelle to get moving again.

At the ranch, she went on in the barn to unsaddle the mare. Grant watched her go. She hadn't said a word to him the whole ride.

He hitched Titan to the rail by the front porch and mounted the steps.

Inside, he followed his nose to the kitchen where something wonderful was in the oven and Marie stood at the peninsula of counter between the kitchen and the breakfast area, rolling out dough for pies. Sliced apples, dusted in sugar and cinnamon, waited in a bowl nearby.

He forced a hearty tone. "How come it always smells so good in here?"

She stopped rolling and grinned at him. She had flour on her nose. "Stick around awhile and you just might get yourself a warm piece of pie."

He hadn't bothered hanging his hat by the door. Instead he held it in his hands. Which seemed sadly fitting. He fiddled with the tattered brim. "Believe me, I'm tempted. But I've got to get back…"

Marie tipped her head to the side and frowned. "Okay. What's the matter? You got a look like someone just shot your best mule."

He swore.

She plunked the rolling pin down and wiped her hands on the apron she'd tied over her jeans. "I'll get you a beer…"

"No, thanks. Marie, I've got something I have to say."

She made a small sound of mingled distress and expectation.

And he went ahead and told her, flat out. "I'm selling the ranch. You'll all have to be out by the thirty-first of August."

What had he imagined? That she'd go all to pieces? Not Marie Julen. Like her daughter, she was stronger and tougher than that.

"Well," she said evenly, after a moment. "All right." And she picked up the rolling pin again and got back to work rolling out that pie dough.

He stood there in the doorway from the central hall and wondered what to do next.

Marie glanced his way again. "Grant. It's okay. It's not the end of the world. Things change. Life goes on."

He almost laughed. "That's what *I* was going to say to *you*."

She pointed her rolling pin at the table. "Will you sit down, please? You're making me nervous, looming there in the doorway like that."

"No, I really have to get back."

"Good enough, then."

But he just stood there and watched her plump, clever hands as she carefully folded the circle of flattened pie dough into quarters, lifted it off the floured board and gently set it in the waiting pie pan.

He remembered that he'd offered her no reassurances. "Marie, I promise you. I'll see you're taken care of."

"Well, of course you will." She opened the folded crust, shaped it to fit the sides of the pan and took up a rolling cutter.

He watched her expertly trim the excess crust from the edge, turning the pan in a circle as she worked. "There'll be another job, a good job," he vowed. "I was thinking you might want to be cooking, maybe something in town, at a coffee shop, something like that..."

She had a second crust ready and took the cutter to it, sectioning it into strips to make one of those fancy lattice-type top crusts that always made her pies stand out for looks, as well as flavor. "Grant." She spoke chidingly, her skilled, swift hands continuing their work. "Stop beating yourself up. We'll be fine. Don't worry."

"I told Steph."

Those busy hands hesitated—but only for a second. "Ah."

"I don't think she's ever going to forgive me."

"You give her time, she'll be okay."

"Damn it, Marie. I don't know about that."

Behind him, down at the other end of the central hall, he heard the front door open. Steph. Her footsteps approached.

He made himself turn to face her, found her mouth set in a stern line and her eyes flat, giving him nothing.

"Did you tell her?" she asked.

Marie said sweetly, "Yes, he did." A glance back over his shoulder showed him she hadn't even looked up from laying the strips of dough in a crosswise pattern onto a floured sheet of aluminum foil.

"You leaving, then?" Steph said. It wasn't really a question.

The thing was, even while she was looking at him with those dead eyes, he still wanted to reach for her, haul her up close, breathe in the warm, sweet scent of her hair, feel her body snug and soft all along the length of his. He wanted to lower his head and crush his mouth to those unwilling lips— until she sighed and opened for him.

But of course, he did no such thing. He said, "I have to talk to Rufus and Jim."

"Don't worry. I already told them."

"Great," he said, guiltily tamping down a flare of resentment at her for taking a job that should have been his. "Still, I want to have a few words with them."

"They're in the barn."

"Well. All right, then." He hit his hat on his thigh. "See you later, Marie."

Marie sent him a smile as loving and warm as any she'd ever bestowed on him. "Ride safe, now."

"I will. He nodded at the cold-eyed woman standing beside him. "Steph."

"Grant." She said his name as if it made a bad taste in her mouth.

In the barn, he reassured Rufus and Jim that he'd find other jobs for them. Jim nodded and thanked him.

Rufus said, "Hell, boy. I know you'll take care of

us. Haven't you always?" He *didn't* say anything about how John Clifton was probably rolling over in his grave at the thought that his own son planned to sell the ranch he'd sweated blood over, the ranch that had been in the Clifton family for five generations.

Grant was damn grateful for Rufus's silence on that subject.

He tipped his hat at the cowboys and left the barn. Out in the sun, Titan was waiting, hitched where he'd left him. He mounted up and got the hell out of there.

Grant rode Titan harder than he should have. He reached the resort in forty minutes. He turned the lathered horse over to the head groom and went up to the lodge. In his suite, he showered and changed into business clothes and went down the hill to the office complex.

Once he'd settled behind his desk, he called his assistant in. She gave him his messages, reminding him that he had an important dinner that night with two of the resort's main backers.

He hadn't forgotten. "Drinks in the Lounge at seven-thirty. Dinner at eight in the Gallatin Room. Right?"

She smiled and nodded. "You have some voice mail, too."

"I'll check it now."

She left him. He played through his voice mail.

Nothing urgent. He checked e-mail—or at least, he brought up his e-mail program and stared at the screen.

Really, though, all he saw was Steph. Her sweet, open face, smiling up at him, eyes shining with admiration and trust. And the way she'd looked Sunday, right after he kissed her, soft mouth red and swollen, eyes full of dreams…

Did she hate him now? Was she ever going to forgive him for the way he'd behaved, for selling off Clifton's Pride when she was so happy there?

He tried to tell himself that maybe, if she hated him, that would be for the best. If she hated him, she'd stay clear of him. It would be a hell of a lot easier to keep his hands off her if she refused to come near him. She'd be safe from him.

He wanted that. He did. He wanted to…protect her from himself—and any other guys like him. From guys who didn't want to get serious. Guys who would steal her tender innocence and then, in the end, walk away and leave her hurting.

The phone rang. He let his assistant answer, but took it when she buzzed him to tell him it was Caleb Douglas.

Since failing health had pretty much forced him to retire, Caleb was at loose ends a lot of the time. Grant listened to the old guy ramble on for a while before finally cutting the monologue short, saying he had a meeting he had to get to.

After the call from Caleb, he took calls from a tour packager and from Arletta Hall. In her fifties, Arletta owned a gift shop in town. She reminded him that he was expected to be at the big parking lot on the corner of North Main and Cedar Street the next day at 11:00 a.m. sharp.

He promised he'd be there, rigged out in the costume she'd dropped off at the concierge for him last Friday, ready to climb on the float and smile and wave his way down Main Street.

"Does it fit all right?" Arletta fussed.

"It's fine," he replied automatically, though he'd yet to take it out of the box she'd delivered it in.

Arletta wanted him to know how pleased she was that he'd allowed her to take charge of the resort's float. "Honored," she declared. "I am honored. And those young people you sent to help me have done an excellent job. I think you'll be pleased with the results."

He thanked her for everything, but she kept on talking. About how well the float had turned out and how excited she was for him to see it, what a big day tomorrow was going to be, what with so many events planned.

"Truly, Grant, I believe this will be the most exciting Fourth of July our town has ever seen. Every hotel and motel is full, and the merchants are doing a record business—including Yours Truly, and I'm just pleased as punch about that, I don't mind telling you. Why, we're a boomtown all over again, aren't we? And so much of it is due to you and the Douglases. That resort of yours has been a real shot in the arm to our economy. We get tourists year-round now..." She yammered on.

When she finally had to stop for a breath, he thanked her for her kind words and gently reminded her that it wasn't *his* resort—and he really did have to go.

"Oh, well. I know, don't I, how busy you are? I understand. No problem. No problem at all."

"See you tomorrow, Arletta."

"Don't forget now. Eleven sharp."

"I'll be there."

"In costume."

"Yes. In costume."

She finally said goodbye, just as his assistant buzzed to tell him that Eva Post had arrived.

"Send her in."

"Grant. Hello." A handsome woman of forty or so, Eva wore a trim gray pantsuit and bloodred lipstick. She carried one of those soft, oversize briefcases. Grant rose to greet her. They shook hands and he indicated one of the leather armchairs opposite his desk.

Eva sat and unzipped her briefcase. She pulled out a folder.

Grant saw that folder clutched in her slim hand with its long, red fingernails and something inside him rebelled.

Sternly he reminded himself of all the reasons he was selling. It made absolutely no sense for him to hold on to a ranch he didn't need, a ranch that never more than broke even, a ranch that stood for the past when Grant was the kind of man who looked toward the future.

But those reasons? They didn't mean squat.

It was no good. He couldn't do it.

"Hold on," he said.

She paused, the folder still in her hand, and sent him a baffled look. "Excuse me?"

"I'm sorry. I've changed my mind. I won't be selling Clifton's Pride, after all."

Chapter Six

Eva Post stared at him as if he'd gone stark-raving out of his mind.

And damn it. Maybe he had.

She tried a laugh. "You're joking."

"No. I'm not." What the hell? He couldn't quite believe it himself. But still, it was true.

He couldn't sell Clifton's Pride. He just… couldn't do it. Period. End of story.

Eva took a moment to collect herself. She set the folder on the edge of his desk and bent to prop her briefcase against her chair. Then she sat up straight again and folded her hands in her lap.

Cautiously she inquired, "Is there…something

about this deal you're not satisfied with? I assure you, Grant, the terms are exactly as we discussed."

"It's not the terms. The terms are fine. More than fair."

"Well, then, what's holding you back?"

He remembered the expression on Steph's face just before he left her that day. She'd looked at him as if she didn't know him at all—as if she didn't *care* to know him.

That hurt. That really got to him. Steph's respect meant a lot to him. It cut him to the core to think he'd lost it.

But losing Steph's high regard wasn't all of it.

He told Eva, "The offer was *too* good, really."

She looked at him as if he made no sense at all. And when she spoke, her tone was patronizing. "Grant. Please. If the offer's too good, why are you telling me you're turning it down?"

"What I meant was, the offer was so good, I jumped at it without thinking it through, without stopping to realize that I really *can't* sell."

"Why not?"

He'd said enough. He stood and held out his hand. "I apologize again for wasting your time." In actuality, he hadn't wasted all that much of Eva's time. He hadn't asked her to represent him until after Melanie had put the offer on the table. "But I'm not selling and that's the end of it."

Eva rose and they shook. He walked her to the door.

Before she went out, she turned and gave it one more try. "You have to realize that Ms. McFarlane is actively seeking the right property for her needs. If you don't respond to this offer and she finds something else that suits her requirements—"

"Eva." He almost smiled. "Why am I getting the feeling you still can't believe I just changed my mind?"

She pursed that red, red mouth. "I doubt you'll get this kind of deal from anyone else."

"I'm sure I won't. But the truth is, I wasn't looking to sell in the first place. Melanie approached *me*."

The realtor refused to believe he meant what he said. "This is a good deal. A terrific deal."

"It sure is. But that doesn't change the fact that I'm passing it up."

An hour after Grant showed Eva out, Melanie McFarlane called. He knew he owed the woman some kind of explanation for backing out of their deal. Too bad he didn't have one—nothing anyone else, particularly an eager and generous buyer, would understand.

Still, she deserved to hear it straight from his own mouth. He took the call.

Melanie wasted no time on idle chitchat. "My

real estate agent talked to *your* real estate agent a few minutes ago. What's going on, Grant? I thought we had a contract."

He apologized for waffling on her and then told her what he'd told Eva: that he regretted any inconvenience he'd caused her, but he'd changed his mind.

Melanie McFarlane was a damned determined woman. "Change it back," she said cheerfully in that brisk New England accent of hers. "What do you need with a ranch? You've got your hands full at the resort and you know it."

"Sorry," he said again. "I know I've inconvenienced you and I regret that. But I'm giving it to you straight here. I'm not selling."

Melanie kept talking. "Your realtor implied there might be some chance you'll be ready to sell, after all, in the near future."

"My realtor, understandably, hates to lose a sale. But she's mistaken. I won't change my mind. And again, I apologize for this. I never should have told you I'd be willing to sell."

"You're serious. I can't believe this."

He did understand her disappointment. Clifton's Pride would be a fine site for a guest ranch. It had a number of interesting, not-too-challenging trails, perfect for novice riders. It was picturesque, with varied terrain and spectacular mountain views. Most important, the ranch house and outbuildings were right off the main highway. To make a go of a guest ranch, access was key. Visitors needed to be able to get there with relative ease.

She demanded, "Is it the price?"

"No."

"I can talk to my banker. I might be willing to up the offer, if that's what it's going to take."

"I'm sorry. I'm not selling."

A deadly silence. Then, "Until I find something else, the offer remains open. I like to think I have good instincts, and right now I have a feeling you'll come to your senses—soon, I hope. When you do, let me know." The line went dead.

Grant hung up and scrubbed his hands down his face. He hoped he hadn't made an enemy of the McFarlane woman. In the resort business, a man did his best to get along with everyone. And she *was* a McFarlane. Her family owned the world-famous McFarlane Hotels.

No, he didn't blame her for being furious with him. Hell. He was furious with himself. He should never have agreed to sell to her in the first place.

He buzzed his assistant and told her to send flowers and a fruit basket up to Melanie's suite, rattling off another apology to go on the card.

After that, well, he hoped Melanie McFarlane would find another suitable property real damn soon and quit waiting around for him to change his mind.

* * *

Grant said good-night to the investor group at a little after eleven and went to his suite.

He started to change into an old pair of sweats, thinking he'd have a drink or two, watch the late news and hope that the alcohol would ease him to sleep. But then, what do you know?

He ended up reaching for his Wranglers instead.

The stables were closed at that time of night. He could have dragged the head groom from sleep with a call. There were, after all, certain privileges that went with being the boss—among them, the right to inconvenience the help.

But as much as the idea of a midnight horseback ride appealed to his troubled mind right then, the Range Rover was faster. And he didn't have to wake anybody to get to it, since it was always ready and waiting in his private space in the main lodge's underground garage.

He made it to the ranch house in twenty minutes flat, pulling into the circular dirt driveway, cutting his engine and dousing the headlights as he rolled up opposite the porch.

For a minute or two, he just sat there, staring at the darkened house where he'd grown up, at the small pool of brightness cast by the porch light, at the bugs recklessly hurling themselves against the bare bulb beneath the plain tin fixture. Bart appeared from the shadows at the end of the porch, tail wagging, sniffing the air in a hopeful way. Never had been much of a guard dog, that mutt.

Grant got out of the vehicle. He shut the car door as quietly as he could and went to sit on the steps with the old dog. Bart sniffed at him a bit and then flopped down beside him, yawning hugely and resting his head on his front paws with a low, contented whine. Grant petted the dog as he pondered what exactly he hoped to accomplish, showing up there in the middle of the night when the house was shut up tight and all sane ranch folk were sound asleep in their beds.

Rufus emerged from the bunkhouse across the yard, long johns showing up ghostly white through the shadows, the dark length of a shotgun visible in his right hand. Grant gave him a wave. After a second or two, Rufus waved in return and went back inside.

More time went by. Five minutes? Ten? Grant didn't bother to check his watch. He just sat there with Bart, his arms looped around his spread knees, knowing that eventually the door behind him would open and a soft, husky voice would ask him what he was doing there.

It happened, finally: the click of the lock and the soft creak of the door as she pulled it inward. Then another, louder creaking as she came through the screen. She shut it with care. Bare feet brushing lightly on the porch boards, she approached and sat beside him.

He didn't look at her. Not at first. There was her scent on the night and the warmth of her body next to his. It was more than enough.

She spoke first. "So…what's up?"

He looked down at her slender feet. "You forgot your slippers."

She made a small sound. It might have been a chuckle. Then she said, "Mom lectured me."

"For what?"

"She told me I was too hard on you. She said Clifton's Pride is your place to sell as you see fit, that you've always been so good to us and I should be more grateful."

He shrugged, looking out at the night again, listening to the long, lost wail of a lone coyote somewhere out there in the dark. On his other side, Bart stirred, woofed softly, then dropped his head back on his paws again. "You tell her how I laid you down on that blanket and kissed you—how I almost did a whole lot more than just kissing?"

She made a sound that could only be called a snort. "Oh, please. She's my mom. Some things a mom doesn't need to know—and besides, Grant Clifton, you weren't the only one doing the kissing. You weren't the only one who wanted to do a whole lot more."

He looked at her then. So beautiful, it pierced him right to the core, her gold hair tangled, eyes a little droopy from sleep, wearing an old sweater over a skimpy pajama top, and wrinkled pajama bottoms printed with sunflowers. "Feisty," he said.

She snorted again. "I am not—and never have been—feisty."

"Right."

"Next you'll be calling me spunky."

"Never."

"You call me spunky, I'm out of here."

"I won't call you spunky. Ever." He raised a hand, palm out. "I swear it."

"See that you don't—and I guess I might as well tell you the rest of what Mom said."

He looked out at the dark yard again. "Guess you might as well."

"She said she can see how it would be hard for you to tell us how you're selling the ranch, because you care about us and you don't want us hurting and you know how much we've loved being here. Mom says I should look in my heart and find a little kindness and understanding there. And you know what?" She waited till he turned his gaze her way and arched a brow. "Now I've had a little time to stew over it, I think Mom's right. I really hate when that happens."

He wanted to touch her—to reach out and smooth her hair, maybe guide a few wild strands behind her ear, to brush her cheek with the back of his hand.

But he didn't. He knew one touch would never be enough.

She said, "See, all I've ever wanted is my own ranch to run. I kind of let myself forget that this place isn't mine, you know?"

"I know."

"So…forgive me for being so thoughtless and cruel to you?" She stuck out a hand. "Shake on it."

He took her hand. Mistake. Because then, he couldn't stop himself from turning it over and pressing a kiss in the warm, callused heart of her palm.

"Oh, Grant…" she whispered on an indrawn breath.

He made himself release her. It was a real hard thing to do. "There's nothing to forgive."

"Oh. See, now. Of course, you would say that."

"I'm not just saying it. It's the truth."

She started arguing. "But—"

"Wait."

"What?"

"Steph…" He sought the words—and found them, somehow. "I'm never going to be…the right guy for you. Whatever we might have together, it wouldn't be a forever kind of thing. I just…don't want that."

"That?" She looked confused.

He elaborated, "I don't want marriage. Kids. All that. I'm not…my dad, you know?"

"I never thought you were."

"What I mean is, I'm not like him. I'm not…the

salt of the earth. Not a family man. What I want, it's not what you want. When I was a kid, I thought it was. I told myself all I needed in life was a chance to walk in my dad's big, muddy boots. But that was a lie. A lie to please him—and to please me, too, I suppose. Because I loved him and wished I *could* be like him. Because the world is built on men like him."

"He was a fine man."

"Yeah. The best. But I'm not him and I never will be. I'm…restless inside, you know? I want to be out there, mixing it up, meeting new people, making things happen. I always knew, deep down, that I had more talent for business than for running cattle. I loved every minute of business school—the whole time telling myself and my dad that I planned to use what I'd learned to help keep Clifton's Pride in the black. But what I really wanted, what I dreamed of, is what I have now. I like the fast life. I like the progress a few around these parts hate. I enjoy my designer suits and high-powered meetings. I like making money. I like being single. And I plan to stay that way."

She considered his words, her elbow braced on her knee and her chin cradled on her hand. Then she nodded. "Okay."

It was a damn sight removed from what he'd expected her to say. "Okay?" he demanded. "That's all. Okay?"

"Yeah," she said, with another strong nod.

"Okay. I don't want you to be anybody you don't *want* to be. And don't assume you know what *I* want. I might end up surprising you."

He had a very scary feeling she just might. And he wanted to kiss her. Damned if he didn't *always* want to kiss her lately. Kiss her, and a whole lot more.

"So we understand each other, then?" he asked, thinking that he didn't understand a thing.

"You bet."

"And I've got to go." *Because if I don't, I'm going to lay you down right here on the front porch, take off that sweater and that tiny little top and those sunflower pj's and finish what I started this afternoon...*

"See you tomorrow, then," she said, with just a hint of a smile in the corners of that mouth he was aching to kiss.

He stood and started walking, putting her behind him where she couldn't see the bulge at the zipper of his jeans. He got in the Range Rover and started it up, leaning out the window before he drove away.

By then, she stood on the top step, arms wrapped around herself, looking so sweet and pretty, it took all the will he possessed not to jump down from the car again and grab her tight in his arms.

"I changed my mind," he said over the low rumble of the engine.

She grinned wide. "What? You mean you're going to come back here and kiss me, after all?"

Her words sent another bolt of heat straight to his groin. "Don't tempt me."

"Oh, get over yourself."

He told her then, flat out. "I turned down that offer. I'm not selling Clifton's Pride."

She gasped then. And she looked at him with such hope. With such gratitude and joy. Like he was Santa come with Christmas on the Fourth of July. "You're serious."

"As a bad case of hoof and mouth."

"Oh, Grant. Are you sure?"

"I am."

She shut her eyes, sucked in a long breath, and then asked, as if it pained her to do it, "It's not… because of how mean I was to you, not because of the hard things I said about turning Clifton's Pride into a dude ranch?"

He answered truthfully. "That was part of it, yeah. But not all. I don't know exactly why I changed my mind. I just know that, when it came time to sign on the dotted line, I couldn't do it."

She hugged herself tighter, rubbing her arms against the nighttime chill. "I'm glad. It's selfish and I know it. But, Grant, I'm so glad."

He found himself wishing he *could* be the man for her. That man would be one lucky sonofagun. And he was going to hate that man when he started coming around. He'd be hard-pressed not to beat the poor guy to a bloody pulp just for living, just for being what Grant could never be.

He brought it back around to business. "You said you could make this place turn a profit. Rufus seems to think you can, too."

"It'll take time. But, yeah. I'm gonna do it. You just watch me."

"Oh, I will." He put the Range Rover in gear and drove away, sticking a hand out the window to give her a last wave, watching her in his rear-view mirror as he rolled around the circle and headed for the highway.

During the drive back to the resort, he almost let himself wonder, what their lives might have been...

If things had gone on the way they'd started out. If the Julens still owned the Triple J and Grant still worked Clifton's Pride at his father's side. If Marie and Grant's mom still sat at the kitchen table together in the long summer afternoons.

If Andre Julen and John Clifton hadn't been murdered in cold blood out by the Callister Breaks nine years ago.

Chapter Seven

The dream was always the same—and much too real. It was like living that dark day all over again.

It started with Grant and Steph on horseback, just the way it had been that Saturday in September almost nine years ago. It was well past noon, the sun arcing toward the western mountains. Well past noon and cool out, rain on the way, clouds boiling up ahead of them to the northeast, rolling on down from Canada.

Steph, on Malomar, her hat down her back and her pigtails tied with green ribbons, was babbling away about how much she hated school. Grant rode along in silence, almost wishing he was twelve again like the mouthy kid beside him. Twelve. Oh, yeah, with years of the school she so despised ahead of him.

He'd graduated from UM the year before. He was a rancher full-time now. And he had an ache inside him, an ache that got worse every day. He missed the excitement and challenge of being out among other people more, of rubbing elbows with the rest of the world.

Steph stopped babbling long enough that he turned to look at her.

"You didn't hear a word I said," she accused.

"Sure I did."

"Repeat it to me."

"Don't be a snot. I got your meaning. It's not like I haven't heard it a hundred times before. You hate school, but your dad and mom want you to go, to be with other kids, get yourself a little social inter-action, learn to get along with different folks. But you'd rather be driving the yearlings to market. You'd eat dust, working the drag gladly, if only your folks would give you a break and your mom would homeschool you, so you could spend more time on a horse."

"I'm not a snot." She laid on the preteen nobility good and heavy. "And I am so sorry to bore you."

"Steph. Don't sulk, okay?"

"Oh, fine." She was a good-natured kid at heart and couldn't ever hold on to a pout all that long. She flipped a braid back over her shoulder and sent him a grin. "And okay. I guess you *were* listening. Pretty much." She pointed at the rising black clouds. "Storm coming."

"Oh, yeah." The wind held that metallic smell of bad weather on the way.

Ahead, erupting from the rolling prairie, a series of sharp outcroppings appeared: the Callister Breaks, a kind of minibadlands, an ancient fault area of sharp-faced low cliffs, dry ravines and gullies. The Breaks lay half on Clifton's Pride and half on the Triple J.

"Wonder what they're up to?" Steph asked no one in particular. "They should have been home hours ago…"

Their dads had headed out together at daybreak from the Clifton place to check on the mineral barrels in the most distant pastures. They took one of the Clifton pickups, the bed packed with halved fifty-gallon drums filled with a molasses-sweetened mineral supplement that the cattle lapped up.

The two men had said they'd be back at the Clifton house by noon. It was almost three now…

Grant and Steph rode on as the sky grew darker.

"We don't come up on them soon," Grant said as they crested a rise, "we'll have to head back or take cover."

And that was when Steph pointed. "Look…"

Down there in the next ravine was the pickup,

half the full barrels traded out for empty ones, both cab doors hanging open.

Grant's heart lurched up and lodged in his throat. "Stay here," he told her.

But she didn't. She urged Malomar to a gallop and down they went. They raced to the abandoned pickup, and past it, up the next rise, as lightning split the sky and thunder rolled across the land.

Below, they saw two familiar figures, tied together, heads drooping, not moving…

And the tire tracks of pickups and trailers and even an abandoned panel from a portable chute.

"Rustlers!" Steph cried.

The sky opened up and the rain poured down.

"Wait here," he commanded. Even from that distance, he could see the blood.

But she no more obeyed him that time than she had the time before. The rain beat at their faces, soaking them to the skin in an instant, as they raced toward the two still figures on the wet ground below.

After that, the dream had no coherence—just as the rest of that day, when it happened, had none.

It was all brutal images.

Two dead men who had once been their fathers, tied together, the blood on the ground mixing with the pelting rain, so the mud ran rusty. He dismounted first and went to them.

Steph cried silently, tears running down soft

cheeks already soaked with rain. "Daddy…" She whispered the word, but it echoed in his head, raw and ragged, gaining volume until it was loud as a shout. "Oh, Daddy, oh, no…"

And she was off Malomar before he could order her to stay in the saddle. She knelt in the mud and the blood, taking her dad's hanging head in her arms, pulling him close so his blood smeared her shirt.

Grant left her there. He took his rifle from his saddle holster, mounted up and went hunting. He didn't go far. Out of that ravine, and into the next one.

Just over the rise from where their fathers sat, murdered, bleeding out on the muddy ground, he found a man. Gutshot. Dying. John Clifton and Andre Julen hadn't gone easily. They'd taken at least one of their murderers down with them.

Grant knelt in the driving rain, took the dying man's head in his lap.

"Names. I want names," he commanded. "They left you here, didn't they, to die? Tell me who they are and you get even, at least. You get to know you died doing one thing right."

And the man whispered. Two names.

Grant left him there, moaning, pleading for help that was bound to be too long in coming, for rescue that would only happen too late. He checked out that ravine, found no one else. In his head was a roaring sound, louder than the thunder that rolled across the land—a roaring, and one word, repeating, over and over in an endless loop.

No, no, no, no….

He saw himself returning to Steph, to the bodies that once had been fine men.

She'd cut the ropes that bound his father to hers. She sat between them, there in the mud, holding one up on either side of her, her braids soaked through, caked with mud and the dead men's blood, one green ribbon gone, the other no more than a straggling wet string.

"I didn't want them tied," she told him, eyes wild as the storm that raged around them. "They would hate that, being tied. But they were falling over. They shouldn't be left to lie there in the mud…"

He knew he should dismount, get down to her, where he could pull her free of death, and hold her. That he needed to tell her some nice lies, to reassure her that it would be all right. Because that was what a man did at a time like this, he looked after the young ones and the females. And Steph was both.

But as he sat there astride his horse, looking down at her in the mud, before he could act on what he knew he should do, she looked up at him and she said, "Get the pickup. I'll wait here. I'll wait with them…"

"Steph—"

"Get it."

"You sure?"

She nodded. Lightning turned everything bright

white. "Just go on." Thunder cracked, so loud it sounded like it was inside his head. She commanded, "You get it. Get the pickup now."

Time jumped. They were lurching through the mud in the pickup, the two dead men in the bed in back. Steph sagged against the window on the passenger side, covered in mud and their fathers' blood. She had her eyes closed. She opened them and glanced his way. He thought that he'd never seen eyes so old.

And then, with only a sigh, she shut them again.

And all at once he stood in the front room of the ranch house, holding his mother as she sobbed in his arms, calling for his father, yelling at God to please, please take her, too...

Grant lurched up from the pillows. The breath soughed in and out of him, loud and hard. He stared into the darkness, he whispered, "No..."

It took a few minutes. It always did.

He sat, staring, shivering, panting as if he'd run a long race, shaking his head, repeating that one word, "No, no, no, no," as, slowly, the past receded and he came to know where he was. Slowly he realized that it was over—long over, that terrible day nine years ago.

Eventually he reached for the bedside lamp. The light popped on and he blinked against the sudden brightness. He was covered in sweat.

For several more minutes once the light was on, he sat there, unmoving, staring in the general direction of the dark plasma television screen mounted on the opposite wall.

He reminded himself of the things he always forced himself to recall when the dream came to him: that it had all happened years ago, that he'd caught up with the other two rustlers himself and seen that they paid for what they'd done.

Things had been made about as right as they could be made, he told himself. There was nothing to do but let it go, forget the past.

Still, though, occasionally, less and less often as the years passed, the dream came to him. He would live that awful day again.

And maybe, he thought for the first time as he sat in his king-size bed, satin sheets soaked through with his sweat, staring at nothing...

Maybe that was right. Good.

Maybe it wasn't bad to have to remember the brutal murder of two good men. To remember how senseless it was. How cruel and random.

Maybe now and then, it was right and fitting to take a minute to mourn for John Clifton and Andre Julen and all that had been lost with them.

To live again his mother's grief and pain.

And to remember Steph. Twelve years old. Taking it on the chin, stalwart as any man. Propping up the dead men with her own young body.

Steph.

Brave and solid as they come on the day her daddy died.

Chapter Eight

The offices were formally closed the next day for the holiday. Grant went down there anyway. He had a few calls to make and some e-mails to return.

Then there was an issue with the concierge. He dealt with that. And head of housekeeping needed a little support with an angry guest who felt her room had not been properly made up and refused to be pacified until she'd talked with the manager. He gave the guest a free night and let the supervisor deal with the employee in question.

It was ten-thirty when he got back to his suite and dragged out the big box Arletta Hall had dropped off last week, the one with his costume inside. He took off the lid and stared down at a pair of ancient, battered boots, a grimy bandanna, an ugly floppy hat and some dirty pink long johns.

He was supposed to be a gold miner—a tribute not only to Thunder Canyon's first gold rush over a century before, but also to the gold fever that had struck two years ago, when somebody found a nugget in an abandoned mine shaft after a local kid fell in there during a snowstorm and the whole town went wild looking for him.

All right. Maybe old-time miners did run around in dirty long johns. Maybe they were too wild with gold fever to bother wearing pants. But the damn thing was a little *too* authentic. It actually had one of those button flaps in back so a man wouldn't have to pull them down when he paid a visit to the outhouse. And in front, well, if he wore that thing by itself around Steph, no one would have any doubt about how glad he was to see her.

Something had to be done. And fast.

Arletta's chunky charm bracelet clattered as she put her hands together and moaned in dismay. "Jeans? But I really don't think jeans are the look we should be going for…"

Behind him, Grant heard a low, husky chuckle and knew it was coming from Steph. "They're *old*, these jeans," he reasoned. "Nice and faded and worn." He'd borrowed them from the groom at the stables, the same one who always had a hat to loan. "And I want to be a more *responsible* kind of gold miner. You know, a guy who remembers to put on his pants in the morning."

"Oh. Well. I just don't think we want to go this way…." Arletta moaned some more, all fluttery indecision. Townspeople milled around them, busy getting ready to play their own parts in the parade.

Grant leaned down to whisper in the shopkeeper's pink ear—she was a tiny little skinny thing, no more than four feet tall and she smelled like baby powder. "Listen, Arletta," he whispered low. "If you think I'm running around in dirty long johns with no pants, you'll have to find yourself another prospector…"

"Oh, dear Lord. No. We can't have that." She sucked it up. At last. "It's all right. Those jeans will just have to do."

He gave her a grin. "Arletta, you're the best."

"Oh. My." She simpered up at him. "You charmer, you…" She tugged on the dirty bandanna around his neck. "There. That's better. And the hat looks just great, I must say—and tell me now. What do you think of the float?"

They turned to admire it together. It consisted of a papier-mâché mountain topped with sparkly cotton snow. A miniature prairie lay below, complete with split rail fences, a creek made of crinkled up aluminum foil, a couple of homemade cottonwoods and some papier-mâché livestock happily munching away at the AstroTurf grass. There was also a log cabin trailing a construction paper cloud of smoke from the chimney and, clinging to the side of the mountain, a miniature replica of the resort's sprawling main lodge. A sparkly rainbow bearing the glittery words, Thunder Canyon Resort, arched over the whole creation.

Grant swept off his hat and held it to his chest. "Magnificent," he solemnly intoned.

Arletta did more simpering. "Oh, I am so pleased you think so." She grabbed a gold pan from a pile of props and also a baseball-size hunk of papier-mâché, spray-painted gold. "Here you go. Your gold pan and your nugget."

He hefted the hunk of papier-mâché. "Hey. With a nugget this size, I don't need this damn gold pan. In fact, I think I'll just head over to the Hitching Post right now and order a round of drinks for everyone, on me. Isn't that what miners do when they make a big strike, head for the bar and get seriously hammered?"

"You are such a kidder," giggled Arletta. Then she chided, "The gold pan is part of the costume— and you can join your rowdy friends at the Hitching Post later. After the parade."

He pretended to look crestfallen. "Yes, ma'am."

"Now, we have to get you in place. And Stephanie, too…" She signaled Steph, who waited a few yards away, wearing a leather cowgirl outfit with a short skirt and a tooled jacket, both skirt and jacket heavy on the leather fringe. Fancy red boots and a big white hat completed the costume. She had Trixiebelle with her, all tacked up in a red and white saddle, with bridle to match. It was a real Dale Evans-style getup. And she looked damn cute in it.

"This way, you two…" Arletta instructed.

The shopkeeper showed them where they were supposed to stand. Trixiebelle, a real trouper, didn't balk once as Steph led her up onto the float and into position and then swung herself into the saddle before Grant could jump up there and offer to help.

As if a skilled horsewoman liked Steph needed a hand up. She'd laugh at him if he offered. And she'd probably suspect that he was only trying to get a look under that short skirt, anyway.

Get a look under her skirt?

Where the hell had that come from?

He was thirty-two years old, for crying out loud. Far past the age when a guy tried to find ways to sneak a peek up a girl's skirt.

"Grant. Are you with me here?" Arletta was frowning, looking slightly miffed. "I need your full attention, now."

He shook himself and tried to appear alert. "You got it."

She pointed. "Stand there."

He took his place by the crinkled foil stream and Arletta stood back to study the picture they made. "Hmm," she said, somehow managing to be both thoughtful and agitated at the same time. "Hmm… oh, no. Oh, my…"

"What?" Grant demanded, beginning to worry that his fly might be open.

"It's too spotty."

Grant cast a quick glance Steph's way. He could tell she was trying real hard not to laugh. "Uh… spotty?" he carefully inquired.

Arletta frowned with great seriousness. "Yes. The composition. It's simply not…pulled together."

The high school band had started to play at the front of the line. "I think we're going to be rolling in a minute or two here," he warned.

"You're right. Action must be taken." Arletta started pointing again. "Grant. Lean that pan against the rail fence. And go stand by the horse—yes. Right there. At the head. Stephanie, let him hold the reins." Steph muffled a snort of amusement as she handed them over. "Much better, yes…." Arletta kept rattling off instructions. "Grant, you'll have to wave with that nugget, hold it up nice and high so everyone can see you've really struck it rich. Do it."

He waved with the fake nugget.

"Oh, yes. That's it. And Stephanie, take off your hat, wave with it. Big smiles, both of you. Big, big smiles." Grant smiled for all he was worth. Evidently Steph, mounted behind, was doing the same. Because Arletta clapped her hands and cried out gleefully, "Exactly! We've got it. That's perfect! Wonderful! Just right!"

And just in time, too. The float gave a lurch and started moving—slowly, like a big ocean liner inching from port. They pulled away from Arletta, who continued to gesture wildly and rattle off instructions. "Wave, Grant! That's it. Wave that nugget. Smiling, you two. Don't forget. Smiling, smiling! That's the way…"

He felt the toe of Steph's fancy boot gently nudge him in the middle of the back.

"What?" he growled out of the corner of his mouth as he waved his nugget high and proud.

She nudged him again, but she didn't say a word. He glanced back at her and she was waving that big hat of hers, smiling wide at the crowds that lined the covered sidewalks to either side. People cheered and stomped in appreciation and kids ran out in the street to grab the candy and bubble gum the driver of the truck that pulled the float was tossing in handfuls out his open window.

Up ahead, the band played "Yankee Doodle Dandy." Grant looked out at the crowd and thought that he'd never seen so many people crowding the streets of his town.

This Thunder Canyon Fourth of July Parade was the biggest one ever, by far.

Even in that silly miner's getup, with the fake nugget in his hand, Grant felt a surge of real pride—that his town was growing. Thriving. That *he* was a part of Thunder Canyon's new prosperity. That his own efforts had contributed, at least a little, to the boom that had started with a modern-day gold rush and continued with the swift and rousing success of the Thunder Canyon Resort.

Chapter Nine

As the float rolled down Main Street, past the charming century-old brick buildings and covered sidewalks of Thunder Canyon's Old Town, Steph waved her hat wildly—and planned her next move with Grant.

Her mom wouldn't have approved of her scheming in the least. Partly because Marie Julen was a woman who found scheming beneath her—and partly because she remained doubtful about her daughter's decision to grab her chance with Grant while she could.

Too bad. Steph was all grown-up now, old enough to make her own decisions. Yeah, she and

Grant had had a rough patch in their new relationship when he'd considered selling the ranch. But they'd gotten through that. Things were looking up in big way.

And today was a day tailor-made to suit her plans. A great opportunity for the two of them to be together, to enjoy each other's company. To have a little fun.

The celebrations would continue all day and into the night. There would be the annual races, right there on Main Street. And after the races, over at the fairgrounds, the big Independence Day Rodeo. She planned to sit next to Grant for the rodeo—except during the barrel races where she was a contestant.

She figured she could leave him on his own while she competed. By then, he'd feel duty-bound to root for her while she raced—especially since the resort was her sponsor and had paid a pretty penny for her top-of-the-line gear.

After the rodeo, she'd get him to take her to dinner. And after dinner, the big Independence Day dance.

She just had to make sure that, when the parade was over, Grant didn't get away.

The problem was Trixiebelle. She needed to get the mare back to her trailer and over to the fairgrounds for the rodeo. But if she took the time do all that, she just knew Grant would find some way to disappear on her. It never paid to give a skittish man the time to have second thoughts. To keep him with her for the day, she'd have to stay close at his side from the moment the float pulled to a stop.

She *needed* someone to take care of Trixie-belle—and what do you know? As the float finished its ride down Main and turned into the parking lot of a local motel called the Wander-On Inn, she spotted Rufus and Jim. The hands stood right there on the sidewalk, at the edge of the lot.

She waved at them and shouted, "Rufus! Hey, meet us when this thing comes to a stop!"

Rufus pulled a sour face, but he and Jim were there waiting when she led Trixiebelle down off the float. Arletta, who'd somehow managed to race down Main through the packed crowds and was waiting when the parade trailed into the motel lot, had cornered Grant again and was gushing all over him.

Great.

She had a minute or two, at least, before he'd have time to make his escape.

"Rufus—"

The old cowboy grunted. "You say my name that way, gal, and I know I'm about to be gettin' my orders."

"I just wonder if you'd mind taking Trixiebelle back to the parking lot at Cedar Street? Her trailer's there, hitched to my pickup, along with my racing costume and barrel saddle. If you could—"

"Hell. Why not?" He knew where to meet her and what time. He rattled them off. "Right?"

"Thanks."

"No thanks are needed—and you better hurry. Looks like your gold miner's gettin' away."

She laughed and paused long enough to kiss his grizzled cheek. "You know too much, you realize that."

"I'm arthritic, not blind. Best get a move on." Beside him, Jim was looking at the ground.

Steph knew the hand was kind of sweet on her, but she'd never encouraged him. She'd always kept things strictly professional between them.

Now, when he finally glanced up, she gave him a quick, no-nonsense nod—not ignoring him, but not encouraging him, either—and then whirled, her mind instantly back on the man who filled her heart. Grant was heading off into the crowd.

"Hey, Mr. Miner!"

He stopped. Turned.

She stuck out a hip and propped a fist on it. "Buy a girl a drink?"

He grunted. "It's barely noon."

She hurried to catch up and looped her arm with his. "A root beer will do." She linked her arm with his. "Love that hat." It was leather, floppy and silly and it made her smile. And he was so big and tall and handsome, even in his pink long-john shirt and dirty bandanna. Just looking up at him had her heart beating faster. He was her favorite cowboy and he always had been.

He groused, "As a matter of fact, I was just thinking about where I could go to change." The good news was he made no effort to pull away from her. In fact, he looked down at her as if he never wanted to leave her side—and hated himself because of it.

She could almost feel sorry for him. If she wasn't so dang happy to be the object of his guilty lust. "You can't change your clothes."

"Why the hell not?"

"Well, if *you* change, then *I'll* change. You know you'd hate that."

A smile tried to tug at the edges of his scowl. "Okay. I admit it. You look damn cute in that skirt."

"Thank you." She shook the arm that wasn't clutching his, making the fringe dance. "It's this fringe, right? You just love a lot of fringe on a woman."

"Er...that's it. The fringe."

The loudspeakers over by the grandstand in front of the town hall crackled to life and over the noise of the crowd, they heard the voice of the honorable Philo T. Brookhurst, town mayor. "Folks, step back off the street now. Time to cordon off Main from South Main to Nugget. We're gearing up fast for the annual Thunder Canyon Races. Get your kids ready to win a twenty-dollar prize."

She let go of his arm and grabbed his hand. "Come on. The toddlers run first. They're always so cute, the way they forget where they're going and wander off in all directions. Let's get us a good spot."

She hauled him along behind her, weaving her way through the crowd. He didn't try to protest, so she figured she had him—for the moment anyway.

And she did. She had him.

He stayed close at her side. He bought her that root beer and they watched the races, every one of them, from the plump toddlers on up to the final race for "octogenarians and above." A ninety-five-year-old woman won that one. She held up her twenty-dollar prize and let out a whoop you could hear all the way to Billings. Then the old gal threw her arms around the mayor's thick neck and planted a big smacker right on his handlebar moustache.

Steph leaned close to Grant and teased in a whisper, "Now *that* is a feisty woman."

"Yeah." He sent her a smoldering look, one that strayed to her mouth. She wished with all her heart that he would kiss her. Right there on Main Street, with the whole town watching. But he didn't. He only whispered back, "Damn spunky, and that is no lie."

After the races, Steph gave Grant no time to start making those see-you-later noises. She asked him for a ride over to the fairgrounds. After all, she told him sweetly, Rufus had taken her pickup to pull Trixiebelle's trailer over there for her.

What could he say? He would never leave her stranded without a ride.

He'd parked his black Range Rover behind the town hall.

"Very nice," she told him, once she'd climbed up into the plush embrace of the leather passenger seat. She sniffed the air. "Mmm. Smells like money in here."

"Smart aleck," he muttered as he stuck the key into the ignition. Before he could turn it over, she reached across and laid her hand on his.

Heat. Oh, she did love the feel of that. Every time she touched him, a jolt of something hot and bright went zipping all through her body. Making her grin. Making her shiver in the most delightful way.

"Steph," he warned, low and rough.

She leaned closer. "Kiss me."

He was looking at her mouth again. "You're just asking for trouble, you know that?"

"Uh-uh. I'm not…"

"Oh, no?"

"What I'm asking for is a kiss." She dared to let her fingers trail up his arm. Amazing, that arm. So warm and hard and muscular beneath the grimy pink sleeve of his long johns.

"A kiss?" he repeated, still staring at her mouth.

"Yeah. A long, slow, wet one." She brushed the side of his neck with her forefinger and felt a shudder go through him. "That's what I want. And I know that *you* know the kind I mean…"

He said her name again, this time kind of desperately.

"Oh, yeah," she whispered as he leaned in that extra fraction of an inch and pressed his lips to hers.

Oh, my. He tasted so good. She opened her mouth and sucked his tongue inside, throwing her arms around him, letting out a moan of pure joy.

He stopped it much too soon. Taking her by the elbows, he peeled her off him and held her at arm's length.

She tried to look innocent. "What? You don't like kissing me?"

He said something under his breath, a very bad word. "You know I do. And if you keep this up…"

"What? You'll make love to me? Oh, now wouldn't that be horrible?"

"You're just a kid and you—"

She swore then, a word every bit as bad as the one he'd used. "Maybe you'd like to see my driver's license. It's got my birthday right on there, in case you forgot how old I am."

"You know what I mean. You don't…date a lot."

Gently she pulled free of his grip. "And you do. I know that. I'm not some dreamy fool, though you keep trying to convince yourself I am."

He actually looked flustered, his face red and his blue eyes full of tender indecision. "I…meant what I said last night, that's all. It wouldn't last. And you'd end up hating me. I couldn't take that."

She held his eyes and banished all hint of teasing from her tone as she told him, "No matter what happens, Grant, I'll never hate you."

"You say that now…"

"Because it's true." She hooked her seat belt. When he didn't move, she slanted him another glance. "Come on. Let's go. The barrel race is up first. I have to track Rufus down and get my horse."

For a moment, she thought he'd say more. But then he only swore again and reached for the key to start the engine.

She lost the barrel race.

Got too close to the second barrel, knocked it clean over. And that was it. The five-second penalty for tipping a barrel took her right out of the running in a race where the difference between first and second place was in fractions of a second.

She gave Trixiebelle an apple and handed her over to Rufus, who said he'd see to getting her home. "Jim can take the other truck back and I'll take yours." He shook a gnarled finger at her. "You watch yourself now. Don't go stealin' some innocent cowboy's heart…"

With teasing solemnity, she vowed, "You know I would never do any such thing." The ranch hand snorted and waved her away and she went to find Grant, who'd saved her a place in the stands.

He threw an arm around her and pulled her close. "Hey, tough luck. At least *we* know you're the best."

She thought that she wouldn't mind losing every race she entered, if it meant Grant would put his arm around her and tell her how great she was. "Truth is, I'm thinking my barrel racing days are over. I just don't have the time to practice like I used to. After all, I've got a ranch to run—not to mention teaching the occasional resort-happy tenderfoot how to stay in the saddle."

He looked at her admiringly. "You're a good sport, Steph. Always have been."

It wasn't the kind of compliment the average woman could appreciate. But Steph recognized high praise when she heard it.

He sat right there at her side through the whole rodeo, from roping to calf wresting, bareback and bronc riding and bull riding, too. It was a dream of a day and she never wanted it to end.

They were back at his four-by-four at a little before five. "Take me to dinner," she commanded.

"This is getting damn dangerous," he said.

But he didn't say no.

He drove to a friendly Italian place he liked in New Town, east of the historic area around Main. He said they'd never get seats anywhere in Old Town, where all the restaurants would be packed with tourists and folks down from the resort, looking for a little taste of Thunder Canyon hospitality.

They shared a bottle of Chianti and she told him more about her plans for improvements at Clifton's Pride. He talked about the new golf course that a world-famous golf pro was designing for the resort, about his ideas for further expansion, about how much he loved the work he was doing.

She grinned across the table at him. "You don't have to say how much you love your work. It's right there in your eyes every time you mention it."

He teased, "Are you telling me I'm boring you?"

"Uh-uh. Not in the least. I like to see you happy, with your eyes shining, all full of your big plans."

He leaned close again. "You do, huh?"

"I do." She raised her wineglass. He touched his against it.

When he set the glass down, he said, "This is nice."

And she nodded. "Yeah. It is. Real nice."

"Too nice..." His tone had turned bleak.

And after that, he grew quiet. Oh, he was kind and gentle as ever. If she asked a question, he answered it. He wasn't rude or anything.

But she knew what had happened. He'd caught himself having a good time with her—in a man-and-woman kind of way.

And that scared him to death.

"I'm taking you home now," he said, when they left the restaurant. His strong jaw was set. It was a statement of purpose from which she knew he would not waver.

Steph didn't argue. She could see it in his eyes: She'd gotten as far as she was going to get with him that day.

Grant let Steph off in front of the ranch house. She leaned on her door and got out with no fanfare.

"Thanks," she said. "I had a great time."

He nodded. She shut the door. He waited, the engine idling, until she went inside.

And then he sat there a moment longer, wishing she was still in the passenger seat beside him, cursing himself for a long-gone fool.

He headed back to town. He wasn't ready yet to return to the resort, where he was the boss with all that being the boss entailed.

Steph's scent lingered, very faint and very tempting, in the car. Or maybe not. Maybe he only imagined it. But whether he could actually still smell her or not, he found himself breathing through his nose, just to get another whiff of her.

This was beyond bad. He'd spent practically the whole day with her. He still didn't quite know how that had happened. Somehow, every time he'd told himself he needed to cut the contact short, she would look at him with those green eyes.

And he would be lost.

He had to face it, he supposed: Steph Julen had it all. The total package.

There was not only her scent and her sweet,

clean-scrubbed face and fine, slim body. There was also that husky, humor-filled voice of hers. There was how smart she was, how charming. How *good*.

She was a good person. He wanted the best for her. Even more so now, when he was finally realizing what a terrific woman she'd become.

At the corner where Thunder Canyon Road turned sharply east and became Main, across from the Wander-On Inn, the Hitching Post loomed. The big brick building was famous in Thunder Canyon history, as it had once been The Shady Lady Saloon, the town's most notorious watering hole, run by the mysterious Shady Lady herself, Lily Divine, back in the 1890s.

Grant turned into the lot, which was packed. But luck was with him. He found a space in the last row as a muddy pickup slid out and drove away.

Inside, the place was jumping. The jukebox played country-western at full volume. Grant knew that later in the evening a local band would be taking the stage at the far end of the barnlike space.

One side was a restaurant, the other the bar, with no wall to separate the two. Grant stuck to the bar side, elbowing his way up through the crowd and sliding onto a stool as another man vacated it.

The portrait on the wall behind the bar was of a well-endowed blond beauty, resting seductively on a red-velvet chaise lounge, wearing nothing but pearls and a few bits of almost-transparent black fabric strategically placed to hint at more than they revealed. The lady was none other than the notorious Lily herself and that painting had hung in the exact same spot over a century before when she owned and ran the place.

The bartender, who knew Grant's drink of choice, set a Maker's Mark with ice before him. Grant dropped his silly miner's hat on the bar, put a few bills down beside it and toasted the Shady Lady just as a deep voice behind him said, "Well, if it isn't the local Golden Boy."

He turned to face Russ Chilton, his best friend since kindergarten. "Hey, Russ." He spoke with a wary smile. In the past couple of years, things had changed between him and Russ—and not for the good. "How you doin'?"

"I've been better." Russ looked around discontentedly. "Kinda crowded in here. Hell, it's crowded all over town. Too crowded, if you ask me."

Grant raised his glass to the other man. "The merchants like it."

"Anything for a buck, right?"

Grant considered trying to lighten the mood with a joking remark about progress, about how change was the only constant. But he decided against it. Lately, it was damn near impossible to lighten Russ's mood. Especially if the subject was progress or change. The man was a rancher, bred in the bone. He liked wide-open spaces and wanted Thunder Canyon to go back the way it used to be.

Russ spoke again. "Saw you in the parade—you and Steph Julen." His dark eyes shone with disapproval. Like Grant, Russ had always been protective of Steph, especially after she lost her dad so young.

"Yeah." Grant said the single word cautiously. He had a feeling he wasn't going to like where Russ was going with this. He tried for a little old-time camaraderie. "Come on. Let me buy you a—"

Russ cut him off. "I saw you with her at the races, too. And at the rodeo."

So much for playing it friendly. "Okay, Russ. What are you getting at?"

Russ leaned in and spoke so no one else in the crowded bar would hear. "Steph's a good kid."

"Yeah. She is. So what?"

"You got no need to mess with her. You got the women waiting in line the way I hear it. Why you want to go and hurt a nice kid like her?"

Russ's words hit their mark and Grant longed to deliver a nice, clean punch to the rancher's square jaw, even though all Russ had done was to tell it hard and true.

But somehow, though his adrenaline spiked, Grant held it together and asked flatly, "That all?"

Russ grunted. "Yeah. That's all."

"Well, all right then." With a curt nod, Grant turned his back on his lifelong best friend.

He sipped his whiskey and counted to ten. In the big mirrors on either side of the Shady Lady's portrait, he saw Russ walk away. Good.

The bartender set a second drink in front of him and tipped his head at a lean, dark-haired man down at the end of the bar. "This one's on the doc."

The doc was Marshall Cates, another of Grant's buddies from way back. Marshall used to practice at Thunder Canyon General, but since his specialty was sports medicine, Grant had lured him to work at the resort by offering a nice, fat salary and a boatload of benefits, including points in the corporation. So now, Marshall was on call to treat the injuries and illnesses of the resort's pampered guests.

Grant signaled him over.

"Russ been giving you grief?" the doctor asked as he eased in beside Grant.

"No more than usual."

Marshall chuckled. "Don't listen to him. He's livin' in the past."

"Whatever you say, Doc."

Marshall sipped his drink, nice and slow, then he looked at his glass as if admiring the amber color of the whiskey within. "I, on the other hand, appreciate the finer things in life and enjoy the fact that I can more than afford them these days."

"Well, good," said Grant.

The two men clinked their glasses. Marshall offered the toast. "To high times and pretty women."

"I'll drink to that."

* * *

Grant hung around at the Hitching Post for a while. Marshall's "little" brothers, the twins Matthew and Marlon, came in. They were just twenty-one, old enough to drink and make trouble—though around town, folks always said that the Cates boys were *born* making trouble. They had the trademark Cates dark hair and eyes and killer smiles. Grant stood them both a drink and listened to them go on about college life—they'd be headed into their senior year in the fall.

Mitchell Cates showed up, too. He was thirty and owned his own farm and ranch equipment company. Mitch had been as wild as any of the Cates boys during his teen years. Nowadays, though, he was kind of quiet most of the time. Women liked Mitch just fine, but Marshall was the charmer in the family. The doc always had a pretty woman on his arm—especially since he'd started practicing up at the resort.

Another old buddy, Dax Traub, who owned the local motorcycle shop, came in. The men commandeered a table and Mitchell bought them all another round.

At a little after nine, the twins headed over to the town hall where the annual Independence Day dance was underway in the main reception room on the ground floor. By then, Grant had had just enough to drink that he knew he wouldn't be getting behind the wheel of his Range Rover—not for a couple of hours, anyway.

He walked up Main to the hall. It wasn't that far and the fresh air kind of cleared his head.

The hall was packed. Up on the stage at the far end, a local band played a fast number good and loud. Grant stood on the sidelines, tapping his foot, telling himself that he wasn't looking around for Steph.

No way would she be there. Right? If she'd been planning to go to the dance, she would have mentioned it earlier. Wouldn't she?

Grant swore under his breath as he watched the fast-stepping, tightly packed dancers.

Okay. The truth was, he didn't have a clue what Steph might do. Not anymore. She was…a whole new person lately.

All woman. Fascinating. Dangerous to his peace of mind in a way no other woman ever had been. So beautiful that just looking at her caused an ache deep down inside him.

He still wanted to protect her—no matter what Russ might think. He *cared* for her. A lot.

He would give just about anything to get her off his mind. And damn it, he was trying to stay clear of her, to forget about her. Not to think about her all the time.

Too bad all that trying wasn't working in the least.

He stood there staring blindly into the crush of dancers, the day he'd just spent with her replaying in his head: the way she'd looked in her fringed cowgirl getup, astride Trixiebelle on the float; the feel of her boot nudging him in the back, making him grin in spite of himself.

Her golden hair flying out under her hat as she ran those barrels—and her good attitude when she lost. Her face across the table from him in the restaurant...

All of it. Every minute of the day they'd spent together.

He hated that it was over. He wanted to live it all over again.

"Hey, cowboy. How 'bout a dance?" Cute Lizbeth Stanton, the town flirt who worked for Grant as head bartender in the lounge at the resort, fluttered her long eyelashes at him.

The band had finished that fast number and started in on a slow one. Why not? If he couldn't dance with Steph, he might as well take a turn around the floor with curvy little Lizbeth.

"Sure." He took her in his arms.

She joked and teased through the whole dance. He teased her right back. They always played it that way with each other, though it had never gone any further than kidding around between them. The spark, somehow, just wasn't there.

When the dance was over, she frowned up at him. "You okay, Grant?"

He lied and said he was fine and Marshall appeared out of the crowd. Lizbeth turned her wide smile on the doctor and they danced away together as the band started up yet again.

By eleven, Grant had gotten out on the floor with a number of pretty women. He felt thoroughly sober. And disgustingly depressed.

He walked back to the Hitching Post and got his car and returned to the resort, where he stood on his balcony and watched contraband bottle rockets shoot up into the star-thick Montana sky.

At a little after midnight, he went back inside.

But it was no good. He knew he wouldn't be able to sleep.

He knew what he wanted. What he needed. He reminded himself, repeatedly, that he wasn't going to get it. He *had* to work off some of the tension.

Maybe a long midnight ride would relax him a little. Wear him out. Ease his nerves and his yearning for a woman he knew he had no right to touch.

In the stables, a sleepy groom emerged to greet him. He sent the man back to his bed and tacked up Titan himself.

By twelve-thirty, he was on his way. The three-quarter moon, turning back around from fullness, burnished the open land in silver, lighting his way. Now and then, in the distance, he heard the sharp explosions of home fireworks, saw the occasional small multicolored starburst break wide-open in the sky.

He rode faster than he should have—at night,

when the gullies and draws are shadowed, a horse can easily loose its footing. But some angel must have been there with him, perched on his shoulder. He arrived in the deserted yard of the Clifton's Pride ranch house without mishap at twenty after one.

He looked around at the dark circle of buildings and wondered what the hell he was doing there. It was not right—not right in the least, that he'd come.

Bart stood on the top porch step, hopefully wagging his tail and Rufus emerged from the bunkhouse with his shotgun, as he had the night before. The old cowboy spotted Grant, waved and went back inside.

What now?

Stupid question. He should turn the horse around and head back the way he'd come.

But he didn't. He let Titan have his head. The gelding wandered toward the barn. And Grant let that happen. When the horse reached the barn doors, he dismounted, opened them and flipped the switch on the wall just inside.

The single bare bulb in the rafters came on. He led the horse in, shut the doors and removed both saddle and bridle, not bothering to carry them into the tack room, just setting them on a hay bale, the saddle blanket, too. Since the gelding wasn't lathered up, Grant let him loose in the paddock behind the barn without brushing him down.

He pulled the paddock doors shut and rested his

forehead against the rough wood, wondering what the hell he was doing there.

Behind him, at the opposite end of the barn, the doors to the yard creaked—and creaked again.

"Grant."

That was all it took: his name from her lips and he knew. He'd been expecting her. Deep down, he'd *willed* her to come to him.

He turned.

She stood just inside the doors, all that amazing gold hair sleep-tangled around her unforgettable face, wearing plaid pajama bottoms, a green tank top, boots and a sweater so big it seemed to swallow her slim frame.

"What are you doing here?" All sleepy and droopy-eyed, she was, hands down, the most beautiful creature he'd ever seen.

In long strides, he reached her. She lifted that angel's face to his.

What could he say? What could he do?

He was lost and he knew it, lost by his own choice, by his own will to come here in spite of his constant vows to the contrary.

There was nothing to say, no denial powerful enough to tear him away from her.

Not now. Not tonight.

A hard, strangled sound escaped him. He reached for her. She came to him with a soft, tender sigh.

He lowered his head and took her mouth.

She melted into him, lifting her soft arms to clasp his neck. He lifted her booted feet off the straw-scattered plank floor and carried her, still kissing her, into the tack room.

Chapter Ten

Steph could hardly believe this was happening—
at last.

After all the long years of dreaming, of hoping,
of wishing that maybe someday, somehow, this
man would see her as a woman, would long for her
the way she longed for him, that he would reach
for her. That he would kiss her so deep and touch
her all over.

Just the way he was doing now.

He kicked the tack room door shut with his boot.
And slowly, he let her slide to the floor.

"You sure?" The two words came out rough and
full of something that sounded almost like pain.

She nodded. She'd never been so sure about anything in her whole life.

The moon shone in the small window on the side wall, more than enough to see by, silvering the space that smelled of leather and straw and clean sweat. Two-by-fours projected from the plank walls, hung with saddles. Bridles hung on iron hooks, reins trailing like black ribbons in the moonlight.

There was a woodstove on a platform in the corner, cold now, but necessary in the long Montana winters. There were stools and a couple of rough benches.

And saddle blankets, some hanging where they'd dried, others folded and stacked neatly on the end of a bench.

Steph went for those blankets. He let her go reluctantly and then he just stood there, like a man in a trance, as she made them a bed on the floor.

Rising, she went to him and took his hand.

"Steph."

"Mmm?"

He asked again, "Are you *sure?*"

"I am," she answered. "So sure. So very, very sure."

Silly man. He should have known her better, should have known that she wouldn't be here, in the moonlit dark with him, if she didn't know in her bones that she wanted this.

Longed for it.

Ached for it, even.

His big, warm hands touched her face, cradling it like a chalice. She offered her lips and he drank from them, those long fingers of his gliding down the sides of her neck, rousing a trail of heated sensation as they went. He dipped his thumbs into the hollow of her throat and a moan rose from her, echoing so strangely inside her head as he eased his hands under her old cardigan. Fingers skimming her eager flesh, he pushed the sweater off her shoulders.

She caught it as it fell, tossed it toward a bench and didn't really care if it landed where she threw it. Because by then, he was cupping her breasts, one in each hand, his hot palms engulfing them. She moaned again then, into his open mouth. He took the sound into him, the way he had taken her tongue, so deep into the wet cave beyond his parted lips.

He sucked her tongue, rhythmically, as he rubbed her nipples, catching them between his thumbs and forefingers right through the fabric of her top, rolling them until they were so hard…

Hard and aching, yearning. Throbbing. In the most wonderful, exciting way.

Her arms felt heavy and between her legs there was heaviness, too. And wetness. Her body wept, hungry for him, though all he'd done was take her mouth, carry her in here, caress her breasts…

She couldn't resist touching him, her hands

skimming downward over his hips. She clutched his hard, muscled thighs sheathed in denim. She caressed him and he pressed himself against her, seeming to like what she was doing, seeming to urge her to do more.

She dared. Oh, yes. She dared. She might be new at this, but she had a bright and curious mind, an eagerness for sensation. And no fear.

Not with Grant. He was, after all, the man she'd always dreamed of knowing in this special way, the only man for her.

By then, he had his hands up under her top and he was touching her bare skin, bringing more moans from her, more sounds that came of their own accord and spoke of her eagerness, of how much she liked every kiss.

Every caress, every tender, needful groan.

She dared some more. To touch him, to lay her hand over the bulge beneath his zipper. He moaned hard when she did that. She sucked that sound into herself.

And then he was taking her arms, guiding them up so they were over her head. In matching long, firm strokes, he caressed his way back down, over her raised forearms, her elbows, her upper arms. She shivered with heat, she reveled in each touch.

He had to stop kissing her long enough to whip the top over her head and off. But that only took a second. Then his mouth was hard on hers again.

And she was in heaven, she was just…lost in a sea of warm, shivery sensation.

In her secret imaginings, she'd always pictured herself undressing him while he undressed her. Her fantasies of making love with him had always proceeded in a certain…erotic sequence: Her shirt, his shirt. His boots, hers…

When she'd lie in her bed alone, enjoying her waking dreams of him, they would always take turns, uncovering each other.

But now, in real life, everything was so much more intense. Wilder. There was no time for order, no taking turns.

He gave her no chance to slowly peel his clothes away, to reveal by sweet degrees the hard flesh of the man beneath. He was a man on a mission and she found she was only too happy to let him lead the way.

Once he had her shirt off, he went for her pajama bottoms. He shoved them down as he lowered that dark gold head of his and took her breast in his mouth.

Oh. My. She clutched his head close to her, little pleading sounds escaping her parted lips. He sucked her nipple, working his teeth so gently against it and she felt a kind of…pulling, a shimmering erotic tug all the way down in the feminine heart of herself, in that wet, hot place that was yearning to be filled with him.

She cradled his head and arched her chest, lifting

her breasts to him, eager for more, as his hungry hands caressed her, stroking the skin over her ribs, clutching her bottom, gliding around over the curve of her hips and inward.

Oh, this…

This was better. More intense. Sweeter than her virgin fantasies. He parted the damp curls between her thighs and he dipped a finger into her wetness.

She still had her boots on. And when he'd shoved her pajamas down, they'd gotten hung up at her ankles, hobbling her, preventing her from spreading her legs as wide as she wanted to. She opened as best she could for him.

And she lifted her hips to him, awash in pleasure, eager for more. More of his endless, deep kisses, his caresses, the things he could do with that bad tongue of his, the way his fingers seemed to know exactly the right spot to touch, to stroke, to rub in little circles until she was crying out, begging him.

"Oh, yes, Grant. Like that. More. Oh. Yes. Please…"

Something happened then. A hot bud of something formed within her. As she begged him to keep touching her, keep rubbing her right there—oh, yes, right there…

That bud became a burning, moist flower, one that burst into sudden bloom.

The hot blooming spread all through her, raying out from the spot where he stroked her. A scream boiled up from her throat—too loud, she knew it, but she couldn't seem to stop herself. He lifted his head from her breast and covered her mouth with his, muffling the racket she was making.

Somewhere way back in her mind she was glad he moved to quiet her.

They didn't need company. Uh-uh. She didn't want her mom or Rufus to come nosing around, wondering what all the shouting was about.

Oh, it was just amazing. She was…swept away. Carried off into ecstasy in a lovely, hot sensation of blooming, her body shuddering with joy, all loose and so gloriously, completely alive.

She opened her eyes.

Well, how had that happened? She was down on the blankets.

He must have lowered her there while the blooming was ending, while she was screaming her excitement into his mouth. She lay back on the scratchy wool, raising her arms, feeling strangely luxurious, running her fingers through her snarled-up hair, stunned with delight at what had just happened.

Time drifted away. She shut her eyes on a sigh, only stirring when he touched her again. He murmured soft reassurances as he pulled off her boots and got rid of her pj's. She was so glad for that, to have her feet and ankles bare at last, like the rest of her. She wanted nothing to bind her, nothing to get in the way of the next pleasure he might bring.

He touched her again—there—where she was so wet and so sensitive. She moaned and moved her hips, easing her legs wider, now that no pajamas reined her in. He touched her, stroking her...

And then his mouth was there.

Oh. Well. Who knew?

Who would have guessed it was going to feel like this? She was swollen and so wet and still yearning, even though a few minutes ago, she'd thought she was finished. Fulfilled. Content.

But now, the pleasure was rising again, her body reaching for more, yearning for...

Everything. Whatever he could give her. Whatever he could teach her. Whatever he would share.

She whispered his name, she told him yes, as she tossed her head on the blanket, her eyes drifting open so she stared, dazed and amazed, at the moon-silvered room, at the saddles hanging on the walls, the benches, the plank ceiling overhead.

He was...doing things. Wonderful things, with that hot, wet tongue of his. She could hardly believe it, the wonder. Of this.

The blooming happened again. Hotter, deeper, more consuming than the first time. She cried out as she had before and he reached up a hand to cover her mouth, to silence her cries of pleasure. She smelled her own arousal on his fingers as the wonder crested.

Oh, the way he kissed her, kept on kissing her, right there, in the perfect spot. It felt so fine, she reveled in it, opening her knees wider, lifting her legs, bracing her feet on his broad bare shoulders…

Bare?

With a gasp of surprise, she raised her head and looked down at him, amazed to find he was naked as she. When had that happened? He'd managed, somehow, to get out of his jeans and boots and shirt, all without her even noticing.

Oh, she was far gone on this, on what he was doing to her. Far gone and more, to have missed the lovely moments when he stripped off all his clothes.

But then again, well, she'd get herself a good long look at him later. When she wasn't so excited. When her body wasn't thrumming with a hunger so fine.

What mattered right now was the feel of his flesh against hers, the heat of him, the hardness.

And her head was just too heavy to hold up. She let it drop to the blanket again, shut her eyes, moaned her willingness, her joy—and his name.

And then he was kissing his way up her body. He lingered to lick her belly, low down, to nibble the sensitive skin over her hip bones.

She lifted her head again on a moan. He was up on his knees, and she saw him…that part of him. So big. So…ready for her. She wondered what virgins probably always wondered: if he was going to fit, and how much it might hurt when he did.

But even as she wondered those things, they really didn't matter. She'd worked around large animals most of her life. She knew that nature had a way of making a fit—no matter how impossible such a thing might seem.

And oh, he was beautiful. His strong body, the muscles flexing. His tanned skin silvery in the moonlight. And that part of him she yearned for? It was beautifully formed, ropy with veins that were visible even beneath the sheath of the condom he wore.

A condom?

Again, he'd surprised her, providing protection without her even realizing he was doing it.

And of course, knowing him, he would always carry protection. Given all the pretty women up at the resort, he'd need to be…prepared. At all times.

He glanced up then. Their eyes met. His gleamed hard and hungry. With a surrendering sigh, she let her head drop, shut her eyes once again—and opened them a moment later as he licked her chin in one long, wet stroke.

He said her name. "Steph…" As if it were the only name that mattered.

All the barriers were down then. She looked into those blue, blue eyes of his. And saw what *could* be, what they could have together. All they might share.

Heaven. Oh, yeah. A little bit of heaven right here on earth.

She felt the rough hairs on his muscled thighs, rubbing the inside of *her* thighs. And the nudge of heated hardness right *there,* where she wanted him, right where he'd been kissing her. Where she was dripping wet and swollen, yearning all over again, in spite of the two times he'd taken her to the finish already.

He braced his big arms on either side of her and he pushed in. She moaned. It hurt. But the pain was delicious in a strange way, her nerve endings so sensitized from his attention, she only wanted more.

She wanted…

To be his in the fullest way.

To feel him, inside her, stretching her, making her give and open for him.

"Don't want…to hurt you…" He growled the words, low. Sweat beaded his brow and the strong muscles in his shoulders bunched with his effort to go easy, to take her slow.

She wrapped her legs around him, opening herself wider. "Now, Grant," she commanded. The command melted, became a breathless plea, "Just…oh, please. Now."

With a deep groan, he thrust in, his hand automatically covering her mouth to muffle her long, sharp cry.

It hurt. But not as much as it pleasured. She moaned and she pulled him down to her, so she could feel the hot, sweat-slick weight of him, the crisp hair on his chest rubbing her nipples, driving her higher, to a fever pitch.

He was still.

She held him. Close. Tight. She took long, slow, hungry breaths and she felt herself relaxing, her inner muscles giving, making more room.

For him. To be hers…

He moved. Another hard thrust.

She groaned low, felt her body opening, taking him deeper.

And deeper still.

He claimed her mouth, his tongue delving in. She sucked it as she surged up to meet him.

"Yeah," he whispered against her parted lips. "Move with me. Oh, yeah. Like that. Like that…"

And from then on, she was lost. More lost than ever. Lost in a way that meant she was also found.

She was a river, flowing all around him as he moved in a slow, hot, hard glide. He was within her and the scent of him was all around her.

There was nothing.

But this. The two of them.

Rising.

His mouth on hers, drinking her cries as the dark flower of fulfillment burst wide into full bloom yet again.

Chapter Eleven

Grant nuzzled her sweet-smelling hair, thinking how he only had one condom left, wishing he had more, but a guy can only fit so many of the damn things in a wallet—and was he crazy?

Was he absolutely stark-raving out of his mind?

He shouldn't have used the first one. And yet, here he was, holding her close, feeling himself stirring all over again, planning to use the one he had left.

Wishing he had more. A hundred of the damn things. A thousand. Wishing he could keep her here, in his arms, forever and a day. Never let her go.

Make love to her over and over. Until the end of time.

He was a real, first-class rat-bastard and that was a plain fact.

"Don't," she whispered.

They lay naked on the makeshift bed of saddle blankets, spoon-style, his body curved around her smaller one.

"Don't." She said it a second time.

He smoothed her hair back away from her ear and trailed his finger down the side of her neck. Amazing, the feel of her skin. Like the petals of some exotic, perfect flower.

"Don't what?" He lifted up on an elbow and she rolled to her back so she could see him.

Damn. He'd never get enough of just looking at her, of marveling at how the brave kid he'd known for so long had suddenly become the most tempting woman he'd ever met.

He was more than just *stirring* now. He was hard again.

She must have felt him pressing against her thigh, because she grinned. Damn knowingly. Was a virgin supposed to grin like that?

It didn't seem right, somehow, that she should be so pleased about this. Didn't virgins usually cry in a man's arms afterward? Didn't they cling and worry and fret over what they'd just done, over whether it was the right thing or not, over if they should have waited for marriage? Or for a different kind of guy?

He'd always heard virgins did things like that. It

was one of the many reasons he'd been real careful to avoid them. With a virgin, a man was bound to feel responsible.

Then again, Steph didn't need to cry and carry on over the loss of her innocence. He already felt responsible for Steph, and he always would.

She was a part of him in a way that had nothing to do with the two of them, lying here in the moonlit tack room, minus all their clothes.

She was…the best of the life he'd once known. She was strong and good, a person a man could count on. She was honest. And true. Willing to work hard to make a place for herself. Expecting nothing. Giving her all.

He wasn't worthy of her and he knew it. He never should have—

"Don't beat yourself up," she chided, her mouth suddenly gone stern. "I mean it." She reached up and smoothed his forehead. "Wipe that frown off your face. It was wonderful. It was…what I wanted. What I've dreamed of. Don't you go and start making it…less."

"Did I hurt you?" There was blood on the blanket. Not much, but still…

She caught his chin in her hand. "Listen."

"What?"

"Yes. It hurt a little. So what? That hurt was nothing, only a moment. The rest felt so good. I'm serious. You will never know how good…"

He pressed his forehead to hers. "Oh, yeah. I know."

That grin was tugging at her mouth again. "Yeah?"

"Yeah."

"Whew. Well. Considering you did all the work so I would get so much pleasure, that's pretty nice. I mean, if it felt good to you, too."

Good? Understatement of the decade. "It did."

She snuggled in against him and his arousal hardened even more. "Well, okay then." She giggled.

"Something's funny?"

Her head was tucked in the curve of his shoulder. She tipped it back and met his gaze again. He saw the naughty gleam in her eyes. "I think you'd like to be feeling good…again." Her hand closed around him.

He groaned. "Oh, yeah. I would…"

"You'll have to tell me how to do this." She gave an experimental tug that sent a bolt of white-hot lightning zapping along every nerve. "I'm not the least experienced." She squeezed. He groaned again. She licked her lips. He knew she did that on purpose.

"It's fine," he muttered roughly. "You're doing just fine…"

They didn't use the second condom for a couple of hours. No need to. She was an eager lover and she wanted to try everything. He was more than happy to oblige her.

And though she amazed him, so adventurous for someone so innocent, she *was* tender after her first time. He tried to go extra easy that second time. But she wrapped herself around him and moved those fine hips so seductively, urging him to lose himself.

He did. At the end, everything flew away but the feel of her slim body beneath his, the wet, tight heat of her all around him. It was sex like he'd never known it before.

Deeper. Better. More…satisfying.

In no time, it was four in the morning. Rufus and Jim would be up and about their chores soon. Marie would be puttering around the kitchen, putting the coffee on, whipping up a big batch of breakfast biscuits.

Steph kissed his shoulder, opening her mouth a little, giving him a quick, teasing stroke of her tongue, reminding him that he still wanted her. Bad. More than ever, now he knew what he'd been missing.

He wanted to roll her right under him and bury himself in her all over again.

But the condoms were used up.

And their night was gone.

Gone, and he hadn't had enough of her. Not nearly enough. He stroked the sleek curve of her arm and wondered if he would ever be through with her, wondered if he could ever get his fill.

She nipped where she'd licked him. "I know what you're thinking, and I don't like it one bit."

He wrapped her hair around his hand, buried his face in it. It smelled so damn good. "Oh, yeah?"

She tugged on the strands. He released them. "Yeah," she said. "You're thinking it's time to go."

"Because it is."

"Stay." She clutched his arm, as if she had the strength to hold him there by physical force alone.

She couldn't.

But she had other things. A face and a body like no other. A scent that drove him wild. A kiss he'd never forget in his lifetime.

And heart. And…history.

They had history together, him and Steph. No matter what happened after this, that would never change.

He peeled her fingers away from his arm and kissed her fingertips. "I can't stay. Your mom—"

"I'm full-grown, in case you failed to notice. A woman with a right to make her own way—and her own choices."

"Marie isn't going to like it."

Steph sat up. She looked down at him, her eyes dark now, shadowed as the night itself. "Don't be a damn coward. We did what we did. It's our business and nobody else's. Can we just *not* sneak around? Can we just…stand tall?"

He caught her hand again, brought it to his lips a second time and kissed it. She allowed that, briefly. And then she pulled her fingers from his hold.

"You're something," he said. "You always were."

"I want you to come in for breakfast."

"It's a bad idea."

"Please."

"More coffee, Grant?" Marie stood over him, holding the pot.

For a split second, he just *knew* she would empty the scalding contents in his lap.

She did no such thing. But she wasn't happy with him. Oh, she acted kind as ever. She'd even hugged him when he came in from the barn.

But he'd caught the looks she gave him—and her daughter—when she thought they couldn't see. She knew what they'd been up to last night.

And she didn't like it one bit.

He nodded. "Thanks."

She filled his cup, went around and filled Rufus's and then took the pot back to the counter. Across the table, Rufus kept his attention on his plate.

Jim kept his eyes focused on his food, as well. Too focused.

Only Steph behaved as if nothing out of the ordinary had happened. She ate heartily and told the cowhands what projects she hoped to get finished today—the fences she wanted mended, the cows and calves that should be checked on because the calf wasn't eating right or the cow had been acting poorly in the past couple of days.

To Grant, the meal seemed never-ending. He ate a pile of scrambled eggs, sausage and two biscuits, shoving the food in his mouth without tasting it or wanting it. The tension around that table did nothing for a man's appetite.

Finally the hands got up and left and Marie started clearing off. Grant thanked her and made his escape.

Out in the yard, he found Titan, tacked up and waiting—courtesy of Rufus, no doubt.

"I guess a kiss goodbye would be asking too much." Steph leaned against one of the porch pillars, arms folded under those small, perfect breasts of hers, shaking her head.

Need pierced him, just from looking at her. She let her arms drop to her sides and came down into the early-morning sunlight and he wanted to reach for her so bad he could taste it. The need only got stronger the closer she came.

He waited, his hat in his hand, until she stood next to him, before he muttered, "Marie almost poured a pot of coffee on me and I think Jim hates my guts."

She wanted to touch him—as he longed to touch her. He could see that in her eyes. But she didn't. She kept her arms at her sides. "You don't know any such thing about Jim. The man does his work and keeps to himself. He never asked me out and I sure never gave him a bit of encouragement. And my mom, well, she'll get over it."

"I hope so."

Her eyes grew sad. "Okay, Grant. See you later, then."

He swore—and then he yanked her close and kissed her. Hard.

When he let her go, she told him softly, "That's better."

He put on his hat, mounted up and rode away. Fast.

"How's the new hand working out?" Marie asked.

Steph turned from the front window and the deserted yard. Beyond the circles of light cast by the porch lamp and the lamps on the outbuildings, all was darkness.

A full week had passed since the beautiful night in the tack room. Jim had quit last Friday, collected his pay and told her he was ready to move on. Steph hadn't asked him why. She'd taken care all along not to get personal with him, and she kept things that way, right to the end. Plus, she'd learned early on that when a cowhand said he was leaving, there was no point in getting into a big discussion over it. Some men just didn't like hanging around in one place too long.

"You need a reference, let me know," she'd told him. "I've got no complaints about your work."

He'd muttered a low, "Thanks," and that was it. He was gone.

Monday, she'd hired the new hand.

She watched her mother knit. Marie could really get those knitting needles flying. She glanced up, over the top rims of her reading glasses.

Steph answered her question of a moment before. "The new man is doing fine. Works hard. Rufus says he's okay."

Marie wrapped the yarn around the needle, hooked it into the afghan she was making and wrapped again. "Haven't heard from Grant, then?" Her mother asked that one without looking up—or pausing. *Click, click, click, click.* The needles flew.

"No, Mom. I haven't."

"You were...careful?"

Steph felt the color flood her cheeks as she thought of those two condoms and how they'd used them, of everything else they'd done that wonderful night. Her cheeks flamed and she felt an ache through her whole body. An ache that had no real location, yet was as physical as a broken bone, a gunshot wound—a knife, stabbing, deep, right to the heart of her.

"Yes," she said. "We were careful."

Her mother never looked up. "It's not the end of the world, you know. Things don't work out. That's how it goes sometimes." Marie spoke gently.

"I know."

"He's a good man. A fine man. But he's not—"

"Can we just...not talk about it? Please."

The flashing needles paused—and then went on.

"Of course. But I'm right here, if you change your mind and want someone to listen, after all."

"I know, Mom. Thanks."

It was almost ten. Time to turn in.

But Steph didn't feel much like sleeping. Lately the nights dragged by in an endless agony of waiting. She lay in her bed, eyes wide-open, listening. For the sound of tires crunching gravel, or a horse's hooves. Noises that meant someone had ridden into the yard.

Since the night in the tack room, those sounds never came.

She turned to leave the room.

Marie said good-night.

"'Night, Mom."

But when she got out in the hall, she detoured to her office, for no particular reason beyond her reluctance to go to bed when she knew she wouldn't sleep. She shut the door and sank into the chair behind her desk, where she stared at the dark eye of her computer monitor and wished she didn't feel so miserable.

Eventually, with a heavy sigh, she folded her arms on the desk pad and rested her head on them. As she had any number of times in the past seven days, she considered going to him.

He wanted her. Bad. She knew if she went to him, she could most likely get through to him—at least physically. Get him to reach for her. To hold her and kiss her and…

But no. For some reason, that just seemed… unfair. To herself. And to him. If they were going any further together, she wanted him willing, for pity's sake. She wanted him *glad* to be with her. She just wouldn't settle for a man who felt trapped by his own desire for her.

And really, the ache in her heart wasn't so bad in the daytime. She had lots of work to do and she kept her mind on that.

And in her practical soul, she knew that no misery lasts forever. The deepest wound either heals—or kills you.

And Stephanie Julen was not going to die. She was too tough for that.

The phone rang. She didn't even jump. It was progress, of a sort. She supposed. Up till now, every time the phone rang, her heart would leap and she would race to answer, just certain it had to be Grant calling to tell her his life was empty without her, to insist that he just *had* to see her.

Tonight, her pulse didn't even accelerate. Tonight, she calmly reached over and picked up the receiver. She put it to her ear and said pleasantly, "Clifton's Pride Ranch. Stephanie speaking."

"Steph."

Wouldn't you know? Now she'd finally stopped hoping, stopped waiting for his call, there he was on the other end of the line, saying her name in a dark, pained sort of way.

She commanded her hopeless heart not to start racing. "Hello, Grant."

There was a silence. An endless, echoing one.

Finally he spoke again. "Look. I really screwed up. I know it. I've been staying away from you, hoping that maybe…" He ran out of words.

She refused to supply them. Except to prompt, "Hoping that what?"

Another pause. At last, he tried again. "That I'd stop feeling like such a user and a jerk. That things would go back to the way they were before. That… hell. I don't know what. I only know I want you. I know if I get near you, I'll just end up thinking about ways to get you out of your clothes again."

More silence. She wanted to beg him to come to her—or tell him to wait right there. She'd break every land speed record getting to his side. And then she'd be more than happy to take her clothes off *for* him.

But in the week he'd stayed away, she *had* done some thinking.

And she'd come to the conclusion that one person can't make love—or even a love *affair*—work. As the old saying goes, it takes two.

He said, as if he'd read the direction of her thoughts, "It can't work, Steph."

"Only because you don't want it to." Her head ached, suddenly. She braced her elbow on the desk and cradled her forehead in her hand. "Listen.

There's no point in this. I want to be with you. I want to…take this thing we have wherever it goes. But not if you don't want it, too. I'm not pushing you."

"I know."

"I'm not demanding anything…permanent."

"I know."

"So then, why are you avoiding me?"

"It's for the best."

Her heart did beat faster then. With anger. She quelled the fury and spoke in a level voice. "I'll tell you what…"

He made a questioning sound.

"Don't call me just to tell me how it can't go anywhere with us. I don't need to hear that again."

He swore, low, and whispered her name.

"Good night, Grant." She hung up.

Chapter Twelve

Since Steph had taken over as foreman at Clifton's Pride, she no longer gave group riding lessons at the resort. They'd hired another instructor full-time. Steph filled in for her, giving private lessons whenever the full-timer had a scheduling conflict.

Steph got a call Friday morning from the full-timer.

"I need you this afternoon," the other woman said. "First, for a half hour with a fast-talkin' guy from San Francisco. Doug Freethy's the name. Computer programmer. Never been on a horse in his life. Then there's a full hour, with a…" The instructor paused. "Ah. Here we go. Melanie McFarlane." Steph recognized the name: the woman who'd tried to buy

Clifton's Pride. "Melanie says she already rides English style. Wants to learn Western." The instructor explained that when she'd spoken with each of the two students, she'd made sure they understood what to expect and what to wear. "So you won't need to make the preliminary calls. Just show up at the stables to meet the computer programmer at two."

As it turned out, the computer programmer was a big, good-looking guy more interested in flirting with his riding instructor than in learning his way around a horse. He asked Steph to dinner twice during that half hour lesson. Both times he seemed vaguely stunned that she turned him down.

"You don't know what you're missing," he told her at the end.

She gave him a pleasant smile. "Enjoy your stay in Thunder Canyon, Doug."

"I'd enjoy it a lot more if I could spend an evening with you."

Steph kept her smile in place and he finally gave up and went away.

Melanie McFarlane arrived at the stables fifteen minutes early. She'd taken the instructor's suggestions to heart and dressed appropriately in comfortable, sturdy blue jeans, a fine-looking pair of Justin boots and an aqua-blue T-shirt. She even had a nice straw Resistol on her stylishly sleek red head.

Steph didn't know what, exactly, she'd expected. But the woman was slim and attractive and seemed nice enough. She listened attentively as Steph ran down the differences between English and Western tack.

They were in the saddle and out of the stable in no time. Steph gave the other woman pointers as they rode. She learned fast. The hour passed quickly— much more so than the grueling thirty minutes Steph had endured with the date-obsessed Doug.

Back in the stables, as the lesson came to an end, Melanie said, "I confess, I had an ulterior motive for requesting this lesson."

Steph dismounted and the groom took the horse.

Melanie asked, "Did you know I plan to buy Clifton's Pride, to create a top-level guest ranch there?"

Steph patiently corrected her. "I know that Grant was going to sell to you—but he changed his mind."

The redhead took off her hat and fiddled with the crease. "I like to think positive. I'm counting on him changing his mind again—when he sees how much I'm willing to offer."

Dread made a dropping sensation in Steph's belly. Was there more going on here than she knew about? "But…he *hasn't* changed his mind again. Right?"

"Not yet. But when he does, I'm hoping you'll stay on and work for me. I'll need a wrangler, someone familiar with the ranch. Someone to give riding lessons to my guests. Seems to me you'll fill the bill perfectly. And your mother—I'll be wanting to talk to her, too. I'm going to need a really good cook. And I do my homework. I know what they say about Marie Julen's cooking. This could end up working out quite well for both of you."

Steph felt sucker-punched. "Honestly, Melanie. The way I understood it, Grant doesn't plan to sell." Her heart sank as she realized she should probably go have a talk with him, find out what this was all about. If he *was* reconsidering the idea of selling out, she needed to know.

Too bad talking with Grant was the last thing she wanted to do that day. Or any day. Not...for a while, anyway.

"I only want you to be aware of your options," Melanie said. "And I don't want anyone thinking they're out of a job. I can probably hire the two men who work for you, as well." Melanie offered her hand. "A pleasure to meet you. I mean that."

After a little stewing over what to do next, Steph went on back to the ranch. She just couldn't bear to deal with Grant for a while—not till she could talk to him without wanting to yell at him. And the more she thought about it, the more she realized she didn't need to deal with him right now.

If and when he accepted Melanie's next offer, she would hear all about it. She didn't much look forward to working on a dude ranch.

But a girl had to eat. And *if* Grant sold to

Melanie, it looked like Steph, her mother and the hands would get to keep their jobs, at least.

She should be thankful for small favors, right?

The rest of the afternoon dragged by. She tried to keep her mind on her work and *off* the infuriating man who wanted her so much, he'd vanished from her life for over a week, only bothering to call once—and then just to tell her how much he regretted the one amazing night they'd had together, how guilty he felt about having made love to her.

That evening, she ended up in the living room, staring out the front window, trying not to wish that Grant would come rolling up in that fancy Range Rover of his.

"Oh, for heaven's sake," said Marie. Steph turned from the window. Her mother had dropped her knitting in her lap. "I can't stand this anymore. Go." She made shooing motions with her plump hands. "Go see him. Work it out. Somehow."

Steph gaped. "But Mom. You said—"

"Oh, what do I know? Except that I can't bear another moment of you moping around here waiting for that damn fool to finally realize he can't get along without you."

Grant stood at the burled oak bar in the Lounge, with Marshall Cates to his left and Mitchell to his right. Marshall was telling some joke about a traveling salesman. He delivered the punch line.

Mitchell grunted. Lizbeth Stanton, behind the bar, let out a musical trill of laughter.

Marshall clapped Grant on the back. "Buddy. You are not laughing. What's the matter with you? You been wearing a long face for days now."

"I'm fine."

Marshall snorted. "Damn. You're gettin' more serious than Mitch." He raised his drink to his brother. "And more serious than Mitch is too damn serious, believe you me."

Grant was just about to tell the good doctor to mind his own business when he noticed Dax Traub coming in the door from main lobby. "Hey, Dax."

Dax approached, his chiseled jaw set in a grim line. Since his divorce from his high-school sweetheart, Allaire, Dax was prone to dark moods. Hell, Grant thought. Except for Marshall, all his friends looked downright bleak today. As bleak as Grant felt.

Steph's sweet image drifted into his mind. He ordered it gone.

"What's up?" Grant wrapped an arm around Dax as Mitchell slid down to the next stool to make room.

Dax shrugged. "Not a thing."

"Pour the man a drink," Grant said.

Lizbeth batted her eyelashes. "What the boss wants, the boss gets."

Grant flirted back out of habit. He sent her a slow smile. Right on cue, Lizbeth slanted him one of her practiced, flirty, come-and-get-it looks.

She set a whiskey in front of Dax. "There you go, Dax."

"Thanks," Traub muttered, hardly even looking up.

Grant got down to business. "You're the man I've been wanting to talk to."

"About what?"

"D.J."

D. J. Traub was Dax's younger brother. He'd left town a decade before, right after Dax and Allaire got married. Left and never returned, except once, for his dad's funeral.

The younger Traub brother hadn't been wasting time out there in the big, wide world. In fact, D.J. had made it big—first by creating and marketing his own brand of barbecue sauce. And then by opening a chain of restaurants, with headquarters in Atlanta. Seemed like everywhere you looked the past couple of years, you saw a D.J.'s Rib Shack. Except in D.J.'s own hometown.

"We need a Rib Shack here," said Grant. "And I don't mean just in town. I mean right here, at the resort. I've been kicking the idea around with Riley and he's in agreement. We want to add a friendly midpriced restaurant on-site. I got a hunch a Rib Shack would be perfect. Hearty Western food, great atmosphere, reasonable prices. And everybody'll love that D.J.'s one of our own."

Dax shrugged. "Maybe so. But if you're thinking

somehow it'll be better for me to approach him with the idea, think again."

"Hell, Dax. He *is* your brother."

"That's right. And I haven't seen him but once in a damn decade. You guys were good friends, back when. I'm sure he'll be happy to hear from you."

Over the years, Grant had wondered what went wrong between Dax and his brother. *Something* had. But Dax always claimed there was nothing— nothing that *he* knew about, anyway.

Grant shrugged. "All right, then. I'll get in touch with him all by my lonesome and see what I can talk him into. However the restaurant idea works out, it'd be great to see him again."

"Yeah," said Dax.

"It would," said Mitch.

Marshall raised his glass. "To D.J. Whatever the hell he might be up to down there in Atlanta."

"To D.J.," the others echoed. They lifted their glasses and drank as one to their missing comrade. Grant couldn't help wishing that Russ could be there with them, to raise his glass along with theirs.

But Russ Chilton would no more set foot in the Thunder Canyon Resort Lounge than he would move to New York City, don a suit and tie and go to work on Wall Street.

Grant plunked his empty glass on the bar. "Hey, gorgeous. 'Nother round for me and the boys."

Lizbeth, who'd been mixing umbrella drinks down at the far end of the bar, sashayed back to them. "Boss. Your wish is my command." She gave him another smoldering glance as she started pouring fresh drinks.

Marshall joked, "Whoa, Lizbeth. Send some of those hot looks *my* way."

She let loose with her flirty laugh as she refilled Grant's glass. "Sorry, Doc. I'm after the boss—and he's crazy 'bout me."

All the men laughed.

"Excuse me. Grant?"

Grant froze with his drink halfway to his lips. *Steph.*

Her husky, amazing voice came from directly behind him.

Every nerve in his body on red-alert, he shot a glance at the mirror over the bar. And there she was. Their eyes met and locked in the glass.

Heat flashed through him. He lowered his drink carefully to the surface of the bar as Marshall and the others greeted her.

"Hi, guys." She nodded at the men she'd known all her life, turning her steady gaze to the bartender. "Lizbeth. How are you?"

For once in her man-crazy life, Lizbeth looked at a loss. She might not know exactly what was happening here, but she knew *something* was. "Hey, Stephanie. So. Um. What can I get you?"

"Not a thing, thanks. Grant." Her voice was cool. Careful. Distant.

He turned on his stool. Faced her. The heat flashed higher inside him. God. The woman could drive him stark-raving out of his mind. Just by standing there in front of him in jeans and a T-shirt, her nugget-gold hair loose on her shoulders. "Steph." Merely saying her name turned him on. And *looking* at her…

That drove him wild.

The night in the tack room seemed to rise up between them—everything they'd done together, all the ways he'd touched her.

He ached to touch her again, to grab her close and slam his mouth down on hers. To strip every stitch off that slim, gorgeous body.

Right there. In the Lounge. He wanted to take her. He wanted it bad.

To have her again, touch her once more, be inside her once more—as he'd sworn to himself a thousand times now he wouldn't ever do again.

Scariest of all? A part of him didn't give a good damn that everyone would see.

He had to get her out of there. Now.

He took her arm. She stiffened—but she had sense enough not to try to pull away.

"Come on," he commanded. "Let's go someplace we can talk."

Chapter Thirteen

Grant had a hold of her arm. A tight hold.

Stunned, Steph made no attempt to pull away. What had she expected when she came to find him?

Caution, maybe. Even coldness. Some stilted reminder that they needed to keep away from each other...

But not this. Not blazing heat and urgency. And the two of them, racing out of the Lounge like a couple of crazy people, leaving all his gaping buddies behind.

He led her out into the vast, open lobby with its huge central fireplace and three-story ceiling. They crossed the gleaming inlaid floor. It seemed to take forever, to get from one side to the other of that huge room.

Were the desk clerks staring?

Oh, it seemed that way. Steph knew her face was flaming and she just knew everyone in the lobby was watching, wondering if the two of them were crazy, or what?

Keeping her arm firmly manacled in his big, warm grip, Grant turned down a wide hallway and suddenly they were walking on lush carpet, their footsteps silent as a breath. People moved past them. Some of them turned and looked. Probably because of the length of his powerful stride, the way he held on to her as if he would never let her go.

And the look of pure determination on his handsome face.

He ignored them all, turning another corner.

They were at the elevators. He punched the up arrow.

"Where are we going?" she asked, her voice small and breathless, her gaze focused straight ahead at a pair of shut elevator doors—somehow, at that moment, she just couldn't bring herself to look at his face.

"My rooms."

The doors opened. The car was empty. He walked her inside and the doors slid shut, closing them in there. Together. They glided upward.

She stared at the closed doors, heat zinging through her. Wanting him. *Needing* him. "You can let go of me now. Please."

He did as she asked, releasing her arm, dropping his hand to his side. Though he was no longer touching her, she *felt* touched. Stroked. Caressed. Her body was on fire.

For him.

She had a lot to say to him. A thousand things. She wanted to understand what it was in him, that couldn't let love in, couldn't give whatever might happen between them a chance. She wanted him to explain himself, to tell her why he found it so necessary to push her away, to keep saying no to all they might share.

That was what she'd come here for: to get it all out there at last, to come to some sort of peace with him.

Peace.

Not real likely. Not tonight.

The doors opened. "This way," he said.

His rooms were on the top floor.

In the living room, the beamed ceiling seemed miles above her head. The wall opposite the entry hall was all window. It faced Thunder Mountain, the snow on the peak blue-white beneath a canopy of stars.

"It's beautiful," she said.

He touched her. Like a blind man, seeing with his fingertips, he framed her face, traced the shape of her nose, the curve of her chin. "What's the matter with me?" The words seemed dragged up from somewhere deep inside him. "I've known you since the day you were born. But now, since that time I saw you by the creek, nothing's the same. Now, just the sight of you is enough to make me lose all control. Oh, God. And the scent of you..." He shut those haunted eyes, nuzzled her cheek, drew in a long breath through his nose.

She wanted to be firm with him. To ask him about what Melanie had told her, to chide him about flirting so blatantly with Lizbeth, to tell him she was angry with him, for cutting her off, for staying away. That she wanted—needed—to understand what drove him to shut her out, to deny her not only as his lover, but as the true friend she'd always been to him.

And yet somehow, as she stared up into his anguished eyes, all that—Melanie's insistence that she *would* buy Clifton's Pride, her own confusion, her suffering at his silence in the past week—seemed nothing. Meaningless. Of no importance at all.

Not when stacked up against the tender, hungry feel of his hands on her face, on her throat, skimming across her shoulders and down her arms....

Sex. Desire. Lust. Whatever you wanted to call it. This power, this pulse of heat and yearning between them—it was everything at that moment. Against the wonder of this, the rest was a pale shadow. Bloodless. Without form or meaning.

Or so it seemed right then.

Later, she thought. We'll deal with all the tough stuff later…

She whispered the single word aloud. "Later…"

He misunderstood. "Now," he insisted as his lips covered hers.

She didn't explain herself. It didn't matter.

He was kissing her. At last. *That* mattered.

Oh, what a kiss. *His* kiss. The *only* kiss. His mouth devoured hers and his hands were everywhere.

He took off her clothes. Got rid of his own.

They stood in the starlit night before the floor-to-ceiling window. Naked. He crushed her close in yet another stunning, soul-searing kiss.

When he lifted his head that time, she opened her eyes. They regarded each other in a breath-held stillness that seemed to crackle with energy. With heat.

For then, for that moment, they were in perfect agreement. She remembered the promise she'd made herself when this started between them: to ride this wild horse wherever it took her.

Right now, with his arms around her, his hard, hot body pressed to her, his manhood thick and ready against her belly, his eyes burning, twin blue flames, into hers—that promise she'd made herself seemed, again, one she could easily keep.

"Steph…" He formed her name as if he had to,

as if the feel of it in his mouth were a necessity to him.

"Yes," she replied, as if he'd asked a question. "Oh, Grant. Yes."

And right there, in front of the window, he dropped to his knees before her. He kissed her again. Intimately. He parted her with tender fingers, tasted her with his tongue. She cradled his head, pushing her hips toward him, urging him on.

In no time, she felt the gathering, the blooming—the hot, lovely explosion that started where he was kissing her and spread through her whole body, so she shuddered and whimpered and cried out his name.

He rose and lifted her in his arms.

In his bedroom, he carried her to the wide bed, laid her down, took a condom from a drawer and rolled it on over himself.

And then he was with her, his body on hers, moving inside her, filling her up so fine and so deep.

When the finish cascaded through them, she wrapped her legs around him. She held on so tight…

They rested.

And then they were reaching for each other again.

She wished the things that lovers always wish for: that it could always be like this. That the night would never end.

Somewhere deep in darkness, content for the moment, satisfied, they drifted off to sleep.

* * *

Steph woke as a sliver of bright morning sun found its way through a slit in the blinds. She squinted at that gold slice of sunlight, remembering.

Last night. With Grant. She moved her hand against the satin sheets.

This was his bed. And the clock on the nightstand read...*6:30 a.m.*

Panic washed through her. She hadn't intended to stay all night. At the ranch, the workday would have started hours ago.

But then she relaxed. Her mother knew where she'd gone. And Rufus and the new man could handle things without her just this once.

With a sigh, she turned over.

And there he was. Naked beside her. As she watched, he opened his eyes.

He reached up a hand and touched her face. So lightly. As if to reassure himself that she was really there. He didn't say anything. And she found she was glad for that.

Yes, there was a lot that *needed* saying. But right now, in the early morning light, she felt much too naked, too raw. Too vulnerable.

She didn't want words filling up the silence. She just wanted...to let the silence be.

He stroked her shoulder. She turned over and snuggled back into him, loving the way his body curled around her, cradling her so intimately, so protectively.

He petted her hair, smoothing it away from her neck. And then he placed a kiss there, on the side of her throat.

She let her eyes drift closed.

They slept some more.

Later, she felt him stir. They made love again. Slowly. Lazily.

Finally, as they lay facing each other, satisfied, she dared to break the beautiful silence.

She laid her hand on the side of his face. "I saw you, last night, flirting with Lizbeth." Her thumb strayed to his lips.

He sucked it inside, stroked it with his tongue. Pleasure shimmered through her.

When he let her thumb slide free, he said, "It meant nothing. Lizbeth and I just kid around. That's as far as it goes. As it's ever gone. A few teasing remarks. A little innuendo…"

"All right."

He turned his head enough to kiss the heel of her hand. She reveled in the velvet touch of his mouth on her skin. He asked, "What does that mean, all right?"

"It means…there's nothing more to say about it. I know you. I know Lizbeth. I get what was going on. That's all."

He scraped his teeth on the place he'd just kissed, bringing more waves of lovely sensation. And he told her, "There's been no one else, since the day I saw you by the creek. I've got no interest in anyone else, not anymore."

Her heart felt lighter. "I'm glad…" She studied his face and had no idea what he might be thinking. He wasn't smiling. He looked at her steadily. She moved on to the next issue. "I gave Melanie McFarlane a riding lesson yesterday. At the end, she told me that she's determined to buy Clifton's Pride from you. That she'll be making you another offer, a bigger one. And when you sell to her, she hopes that my mom and Rufus and the new hand and I will stay on to work at her dude ranch."

"But I'm not selling to her."

"Seriously, she did mention a larger offer. And I know that the first one must have been pretty good for you to have even considered it…"

"It doesn't matter what she offers. I'm keeping Clifton's Pride. And I'll talk to her. Again. This time I'll make sure that we understand each other."

Steph hadn't realized she was holding her breath. She let it out slowly. "Good." And now came the hard part. "I'm sorry," she said. "I thought…I could just go with this, with you and me. Just kind of take it however it happened."

"But you can't."

She smiled a sad smile. "You say it like you knew that all along."

He made a low sound, something midway between a grunt and a chuckle. "Because I did."

She said, "This last week. It's been awful."

He said nothing for a moment. She waited, letting him consider his response. At last, he told her, "I thought it would be the best thing…to break it off. You know. Cut it clean. I tried to explain it on the phone. Didn't do a very good job of it."

"You seem…"

He caught her thumb between his lips again, licked the fleshy pad, let it go. "I seem what?"

"Oh, Grant. I don't know. Resigned, maybe? Yeah. That's it. You seem resigned."

He ran a finger along the outside of her arm, bringing a trail of goose bumps, sending a hot little thrill down to her core. "When I saw you last night, in the Lounge, I knew it was hopeless." Hopeless? Such a strange word to choose. "I knew I couldn't give you up."

"Give me up? You say it like you wish you could, like I'm some kind of liquor or bad drug you've gone and gotten yourself addicted to."

"Steph. What do you want me to tell you? I *do* wish I could give you up. It would be better if I could. Better if, over time, we could go back the way we used to be."

"But…it's not what it used to be. It never will be again."

"It doesn't matter, anyway. The fact is I can't. I've never felt like I feel about you."

"And that's bad?"

"I never wanted to feel this way. I like a life that's…uncomplicated, you know? I like my freedom. But I'm not free. Not anymore. Even if I managed to walk away from you, it would kill me inside. And if you found someone else…" He shook his head. "I've thought about that. A lot in the past two weeks. How you should find someone else. How it would be better for you if you did—and how, if you did, I'd spend my life hating that other man's guts and wishing him dead. For doing nothing—but loving you better than I ever could."

She sat up then, and gathered the sheet around herself. "You make it sound like such a terrible thing. To want to be with me. To miss me when we're apart."

"I'm sorry. I'm making a mess of this. As usual."

"I didn't say that…"

"Look. However I made it sound, it's…how it is. And like I said, I know how you are. You're not a woman to be taken lightly. When you give, you give it all. I won't disrespect you. Not anymore."

"Grant. No. You don't understand. You haven't disrespected me. Never. No way."

"But I know what you want. And I accept it." He reached up, hooked his hand around the back of her neck and pulled her down to him again. Eye to eye with her, he said, "We'll get married. It's the best way."

Chapter Fourteen

Surely she hadn't heard him right. "Grant?"

"What?"

"Married? Did you say…married?"

"Yeah." He kissed her cheeks, pressing his soft lips first to one and then the other. "Get together with your mom. Figure out how you want to handle it. Whatever you decide, weddingwise, it's fine with me. Make it soon, that's all I ask."

She pulled away from him and grabbed the sheet close again. Her throat had clutched up. She had to cough to clear it. "But I don't…you're not serious."

"Yeah. I am."

"Marriage? *Now?*"

He sat up, too. "Don't look so shocked. It is what you wanted, right?"

For all of my life…

But, oh. Not like this. Not so…grimly. Not as if he hated the very idea, as if he were somehow resigned to his fate.

"It's too soon," she said.

His brow creased and that mouth she loved to kiss turned down at the corners. "Too soon for what?"

"For us. To get married. We're not ready yet."

"We're as ready as we'll ever be."

"No. We're not. Two weeks ago, you thought of me as a sort of honorary kid sister. Everything's changing between us. I think that's good. It's what I've always dreamed of, longed for. But marriage… no. Uh-uh. Not yet."

He gave her a long, hooded look. "It's the words of love, right?"

"Pardon me?"

"You want me to tell you I love you. All right. I love you. I can't live without you. It's driving me crazy, wanting you all the time. Put me out of my misery. Marry me."

"Oh, Grant. Just listen to yourself. Put you out of your *misery?* Like a pony that's come up lame?"

He scowled. "I'm spilling my guts here and you're making jokes about it."

"No. I'm not. I'm just trying to get you to see.

It's not something we should rush. We need to… know each other better."

"You've known me all your life."

"Not like this. Not in a man and woman way. This is…it's like getting to know each other all over again."

He slumped back against pillows. "You're mad at me now."

"No. I swear. I'm not."

"I've made this too cut-and-dried. I'm sorry. It's difficult for me and I—"

"Grant. I'm not mad. And if I thought we were ready for marriage right now, I wouldn't care how you asked me. I'd be saying yes."

"You don't want to marry me?" He looked like she'd just dropped a boulder on his head.

"But I do."

"Then why the hell do you keep saying no?"

She took his hand. He let her have it, but his eyes were watchful, doubtful. On guard. "I'm just going to say this. Just…say it right out and clear the air, okay?"

"Damn it, Steph. What?"

She barreled into it, before she could lose her nerve. "I love you, Grant Clifton. I'm *in* love with you. I think I always have been, ever since I was kid. I never planned to tell you what was in my heart. I never figured that you would—or could— love me back. But then, after that day by the creek, after the first time you kissed me…I started to hope.

All at once, you were seeing me as a woman. You wanted me. And, well, suddenly, it seemed like anything might happen. All my dreams might just come true."

"So, fine." He brought her hand to his lips and kissed the back of it. "Marry me." He licked where he'd kissed.

And she was so tempted. To do whatever he wanted. To say yes. Yes, yes, yes! To head for the altar, and work the problems out later.

But she couldn't. To her, marriage was a sacred promise. A lifetime agreement a person needed to be ready for. "Oh, why can't you see? For marriage, there has to be more than just not being able to keep our hands off each other. There has to be easiness between us. We need to be each other's best friend. There's got to be trust, a knowledge that we're in understanding with each other. About what we want out of life, about what kind of life we're going to live. You know what I mean. Your folks had it. So did mine."

He pulled his hand from hers. "It's that damn ranch, isn't it? You want me to give up the resort business and move back to Clifton's Pride."

She tamped down a surge of frustration. "No. I don't want you to give up the work you love. Why would I want that? That's not what I meant."

"Good," he growled. "Because it's not happening."

"I know that. And Grant. That you *don't* know I know that…that's why we need more time."

He stared at her. And he didn't look happy. "You're talking in circles. The truth is, you're not sure you want to marry me."

"Wrong. I'm sure. I'm just not ready."

He swore and then he swore some more. "There you go. Talking in circles, like I said. If you're not ready, it's because you're not sure."

She sat a little straighter. "This is going nowhere."

"Because you won't be straight with me."

"That's not so. And you're not going to bully me into this, so you can just save your breath on that score."

"Yes or no, Steph. It's simple. Yes or no."

She couldn't sit still. So she threw back the covers. But then she realized her clothes were in the other room. She flipped the sheet back over herself and demanded, "Are you trying to chase me away? Is that it?"

His jaw was as set as a slab of granite. "Yes or no?"

She longed to pop him a good one about then. Somehow, though, she controlled herself. The way he was acting only proved her point. But that didn't mean he would let himself see it.

His blue eyes shone hard and bright as he repeated his ultimatum. "Yes or no. Make up your mind."

Oh, she knew what he was doing. He'd boxed

her in neatly: She said yes when she wasn't ready to—or she rejected him. Either way, as far as she was concerned, they would both lose.

"Yes or no."

And it came to her. A workable response. "Yes. In December."

He gaped. And then another string of swear words turned the air blue.

"Why are you swearing at me? I said yes."

"In damn December?"

"That's right. At Christmas time. It's not that long." But it *was* long enough that maybe they could work a few things out. Maybe he'd open up to her more. Maybe, by then, they would be friends again.

Oh, how she longed for that. She wanted him so bad. Just plain lusted like mad for him.

She loved him with all her yearning heart.

But he wasn't her friend anymore. And the man that she married *would* be her friend.

"December," he muttered, as if the word tasted bad in his mouth. But then he grabbed her and kissed her and she knew that though he didn't like it, he would do this her way.

That afternoon, Grant called his mother in Billings. He told her that he and Steph were getting married.

Helen Clifton congratulated him. She said, "I always had a feeling you and little Steph would get together."

"Hell, Ma. You did? You never said a word to me."

"And have you tell me I was crazy? I don't think so."

He told her they hadn't set a date yet. "Sometime in December, I think." *Unless I can get her to quit stalling and see things my way.*

"December," said his mother in a musing tone. "It's a fine month for a wedding…"

He made a low, disagreeable sound. As much as he hated the way Steph was stalling him, he didn't want to get into it with his mom.

She said, "Keep us posted, will you?"

"We will." He dared to add, "I hope you'll come."

After a moment, she promised, "We'll be there. You and Steph. A December wedding. How could your sister and I miss that?"

He was pleased. And more than a little surprised. His mother didn't like to return to Thunder Canyon. For her, there were too many sad memories waiting there.

Grant drove out to the ranch that evening so he and Steph could tell Marie their big news.

Marie hugged them both and said she was sure they'd be really happy together. Grant had a funny feeling Steph's mom had reservations about the engagement, but she didn't say so and he had no intention of asking her what she *really* thought. Marie had two lips and a voice box and a fine command of the English language. If she had objections, it was up to her to speak them out loud and clear.

Grant didn't get it. Not any of it. Not Marie's lukewarm reaction to the news. And not Steph.

He didn't get Steph in the least. She said she loved him. That she'd *always* loved him.

But she wasn't going to marry him for months.

Damn it. Now he was resigned to being her husband, he wanted it done. He'd never been a man to drag out the inevitable.

If Marie seemed kind of lukewarm at the news, Rufus was downright ecstatic. He clapped Grant on the back and told him what a lucky man he was and then insisted Marie get out the good Scotch so they could share a toast—or three—to love and happiness.

After dinner, Grant and Steph went out and sat on the front steps in the warm evening.

He put his arm around her and she snuggled in close and he breathed in the arousing scent of her and wished they were at the resort, in his bed. Where he could touch every inch of her, bury himself inside her, hold her close to his body all night long.

He pressed his lips to her silky hair. And grumbled, "You thought about how we're gonna sleep together when we're married? I work late most nights—and you're up and in the barn at five in the morning."

"Hey."

"What?" He growled the word.

"Get that chip off your shoulder. It's all going to work out."

"It's a problem."

"We'll manage. It's less than half hour by car between here and the main lodge. Some nights I'll be there, with you. And some nights you can come here."

"Oh. Yeah. So damn simple."

She turned her head and pressed her lips against his neck, thrilling him. Her every damn touch just set him on fire. "Shh. Don't be a grump. Please."

He tipped her chin up and kissed her. Harder and deeper than he should have maybe, considering they sat right out there on the porch where anyone might glance out a window and see what they were up to. When he finally lifted his head, she gazed at him kind of wistfully. He didn't ask her why the sad look. Hell. If he asked, she'd be sure to tell him and he might not like what she had to say.

They sat in silence for a time. Bart's back leg thumped the porch as he scratched himself behind the ear. Somewhere beyond the circle of the buildings, an owl hooted. From the bunkhouse, faintly, Grant heard music. Rufus was playing his old Johnny Cash tapes on that ancient boom box of his.

Grant wasn't going to bring Marie up—but he

heard himself doing it anyway. "Your mom doesn't seem all that excited about us getting married."

Steph looked at him levelly. "I think she has doubts it's what you really want."

That irked him. "What *I* really want? I'm not the one who's put the wedding off till Christmas. You tell her that?"

"You were there. You heard what I said." He wasn't the only one who was irritated. Those green eyes flashed. "And if you've got a problem with my mom's reaction, maybe you ought to have a talk with her about it."

He realized they were on the verge of an argument. Now, how the hell had that happened? "Look. I don't want to fight."

"Could have fooled me." She muttered the words as she turned her head away.

He wanted to grab her close. Kiss her some more. But then he wouldn't want to stop with just kissing. And *then* what would they do? Head for the tack room and make love on the rough wood floor again? March upstairs together, right past Marie sitting in the living room with her knitting? He wouldn't feel right about that. It would seem…disrespectful to the woman who had been his mother's best friend. And to Steph, too, somehow.

Damn it. Why did this have to be so complicated?

Because Steph just had to wait five months before she'd wear his wedding ring.

He stood. "I think I'd better go."

She rose, too. "Good night, then." She didn't look annoyed anymore. She didn't look particularly adoring, either, like a bride-to-be ought to. What she looked was self-contained. Distant. Accepting.

He reached down and took her hand and pulled her up into the circle of his arms. She softened as he kissed her. And then she walked him the few steps to the Range Rover. He got in.

She shut the door. "Thank you for the ring." The big engagement diamond glittered on her tanned hand. He'd made a special trip to Billings that afternoon to buy it. He'd even guessed her size right. "It's beautiful," she added, sounding like she meant it. "I'll treasure it always."

He took that hand with the ring on it, turned it over and pressed a card key into her palm. "To my suite."

Her cheeks colored. With pleasure, he hoped. "Thank you."

He wanted to demand she come to him tomorrow night. But what if she said she couldn't, that she had too much work on her hands at the ranch? His pride was ragged enough, with the way she'd put off marrying him. He didn't need to know he took second place to a broken fence or a sick cow.

She stepped back from the vehicle and he drove away.

Since it was still early and he didn't much relish the thought of going back to his empty rooms at the resort, he stopped in at the Hitching Post in town.

Dax, Marshall, Mitchell, the twins and Russ were there, playing Texas hold 'em in the back. They all got together to play at least once a month, usually around the first. But with all the Independence Day hoorah that month, they'd put it off till now. Grant grabbed a chair and joined them. He won four hands in a row.

Marshall remarked that he was looking pretty grim for a guy on a winning streak.

Grant only shrugged and nudged Mitchell to his left. "Deal."

Mitch obliged. Grant tipped up the corners of his two hole cards. Big Slick—an ace and a king. His luck was holding. He bet twenty and then got two more aces on the flop. In two more rounds of betting, he coaxed more money out of them. Then, on the river, he went all in.

The rest of them folded.

He was hauling in his winnings when Russ said, "I heard you're selling Clifton's Pride."

He gave Russ a look. Not a friendly one. "Who told you that?"

Russ shrugged. "Word gets around."

Melanie McFarlane.

The woman must have been talking to more than just Steph. *Tomorrow,* Grant thought. Without fail. He would have a talk with Melanie and make certain she understood that he was never going to sell her Clifton's Pride.

He told Russ, "You heard wrong. I'm keeping the ranch."

"Well." For the first time in two years, Russ looked at him without a scowl. "Good. It's a fine spread. I'd hate to see you let it go."

"What could I do? My fiancée is set on keeping the place. And you know women. What they want, they get."

The table went dead still.

Marshall said, "What the hell? Your *fiancée?*"

Dax said, "Stephanie, right? You and Stephanie…"

Grant nodded. "That's right."

Mitchell let out a low laugh. "Damn. Never in a million years would I have guessed you'd be the first of us to tie the knot."

"Steph wants a December wedding." Grant tried not to sound as bugged as he felt over the way she'd put him off for almost half a year when, to him, the whole point of the marriage was to get things settled between them. "That's months from now. So who knows? Maybe one of you will beat me to the altar, after all."

They all laughed at that one. And Mitchell faked a threatening glare. "We're gonna have to pretend you didn't say that."

Dax grunted. "Yeah. Otherwise, we'd have to kill you."

A rumble of agreement went around the table.

"We're single men," Marshall announced to the table at large. "And we like it that way." He looked at Grant again. "You and Steph. Hell. Life is just packed with surprises, and that is no lie."

And then they were all out of their seats, even Russ, gathering around his chair, pounding him on the back and telling him what a lucky man he was, razzing him about how brave he was, taking on a woman full-time, for life.

He let it go on for a minute or two.

Then he commanded, "Enough. Take your seats. Let's get back down to business here, boys. When I head for the resort tonight, I plan on taking all your money with me."

Grant called Melanie in her rooms at nine the next morning and asked if she was free for lunch.

"I am," she answered briskly.

"The Gallatin Room at one?"

"I'll see you there."

He arrived fifteen minutes early and was waiting at a prime table by the fireplace when she arrived. She waved away an offer of a cocktail and told the waiter she'd have a Caesar salad and an iced tea.

The waiter turned to him. "Mr. Clifton?"

"The usual. Thanks, Paul."

The waiter nodded and left them, reappearing in no time with a basket of hot bread and Melanie's tea.

Grant wished for a nice, stiff whiskey. He sipped his water. "How's the property hunt going?"

She opened her designer bag and took out a pen and a small square of paper. "I've been meaning to talk to you about that."

"You have, huh? Well, I wouldn't say I'm an expert on what to buy and how much to pay, but I do know the area. I'll be glad to tell you what I've heard about any of the spreads up for sale around here."

"Grant." She said his name patiently. "Don't play me."

"Well, Melanie. I'm not the one who's doing the playing around here."

She wrote on the paper. "I'm not sure I made this clear before, but I'm financing my guest ranch project out of my own funds. Whatever you may have heard about my family money and connections, I'm on my own now. I can pay well, but my pockets are only so deep. That said, I'm determined to make a success here in Thunder Canyon. And I want Clifton's Pride. I want it a lot." Her dark eyes shone with a steely resolve.

Well, well. Melanie McFarlane might be a rich city gal, but damned if she didn't have more than her share of grit. Grant found himself believing that she would succeed at anything she set that sharp mind to.

However, she wasn't getting Clifton's Pride. "I wish you the best of luck. I'm sure you'll do just fine."

She picked up the scrap of paper and set it down

again—directly in front of him. "There's my final offer. Say yes now and I'll have my realtor draw up the new contract today."

Grant glanced down and almost let out a whistle. The figure was a lot more than her first offer, and that had been a fine one. He met her eyes. "I don't know how to make this any clearer than I already have. I'm really sorry you've got your heart set on my ranch, because I meant what I said the last time we talked."

"But—"

He raised a hand. "You're wasting your breath, Melanie. I'm not selling."

"I'm sure you—"

"I'll say it again. No. No matter what you offer, I'm keeping my ranch. I've realized Clifton's Pride isn't something I can let go of, after all. Plus, my fiancée is damned fond of the place."

Melanie blinked. "Your…fiancée? I didn't know you were engaged."

"I am. To Stephanie Julen. You know, my foreman? The one you offered a job to day before yesterday?"

"Oh. Well…" The redhead swallowed. Hard.

"I'd appreciate it if you'd stop offering jobs to the people who work for me."

"I only thought it might be reassuring for them to know—"

"They don't need reassurances. They already have jobs. They work for me."

"It wasn't my intention to offend."

"I'm not offended. I'm also not selling. I'll keep my eyes and ears open for you, though, like I said I would. If I hear of something that might suit your needs, I'll let you know. *I'd* like to know that you're hearing me loud and clear this time. I'm not selling my ranch and that's my final word on the subject."

Melanie put her hands in her lap and sat very straight. After a moment, she granted him a regal nod. "All right."

"I hate to belabor this point, but I need to know for certain that you're going stop running around town telling everybody you talk to that you're buying my ranch."

"I get it. You're not selling. That's firm. And I think I've lost my appetite." She tucked her napkin in beside her untouched iced tea and rose. "Excuse me."

He watched her walk away from the table with her red head high. He still felt bad about backing out of the deal with her, especially now that he was coming to admire her gumption.

But he'd accomplished his goal with her, at least. She finally understood that she would have to look elsewhere for the property she needed to build that dude ranch of hers.

Steph surprised him that night.

She did come to see him.

In fact, she was asleep in his bed when he got

up to his suite at ten. She'd left a lamp on low across the room, so he wouldn't have to stumble around in the dark.

He stood over her, captivated by the sight of her in his bed.

She lay on her side, her hand tucked under her head. He was mesmerized—by the inward curve of her waist and the smooth swell of her hip under the sheet, by the shadowed luster of her skin. Her hair, like gold silk, flowed back from her head against the white satin pillow. She was so beautiful it made a sharp ache down inside him, just to look at her.

She stirred and rolled onto her back. Her eyes opened. And she smiled. "There you are." She reached up those slim arms.

He couldn't get out of his clothes fast enough.

She held the sheet up for him, welcoming him. He went down to her softness. And she touched him, bringing a deep, hungry groan from him as her strong fingers encircled him.

Lost, he thought, as she stroked him. *I'm gone. Finished. Hers...*

She kissed him. Deeply. He surrendered to her caresses, to the giving, wet softness of her mouth under his.

When he fumbled for the condom, she got to it first. She rolled it down over him. Slowly. He groaned some more as she rose up over him, straddling him, taking him into her by slow degrees.

He looked up at her, watching her as she rode him, her body moving like a wave above him, her hair falling forward, brushing his chest when she bent down to kiss him. He wrapped his arms around her and pulled her down.

She came to him willingly, gave herself completely. Eagerly. As if surrendering to him was the most natural thing, as if giving him everything only made her *more*.

She didn't understand. It wasn't that easy for him. His whole life was changed, now, because of her.

His mind, all his senses, every beat of his heart. All of him. Hers. There would never be another for him.

He knew that now.

It wasn't what he'd wanted for himself. It scared him, to belong to someone the way he belonged to her, scared him to want someone as much as he wanted her.

What would happen if he lost her?

How would he live if she was gone?

No answer came.

And soon enough, the pleasure claimed him, pushing all the dark questions from his mind. He crushed her close and surged up into her as his climax rolled through him, stealing all thought.

Chapter Fifteen

Patience, Steph told herself. *I need to be patient with him.*

Yet as one gorgeous summer day became the next, she couldn't help getting a little discouraged. She went to him every chance she got. Most nights, she would be there, waiting, when he came to his rooms at the resort.

He made love to her with a passion and a heat that continued to astound and amaze her. And though he had a well-deserved rep as a ladies' man, she had no trouble believing that he'd put the bachelor life behind him. He wanted her and only her. She had zero complaints on that score.

But he was still angry that she insisted on waiting until December for the wedding. Every chance he got, he tried to push her to move the date closer.

More than once, he suggested they just run off to Las Vegas.

And then she would say how she really did want to wait. And he would get surly.

She kept hoping he would…what?

Relax a little, maybe? Not be so guarded and gruff. She wasn't the kind who needed a man to talk to her constantly. She had no problem at all with silence—not as long as it was a good silence, one without anger or bitterness, one sweet and easy with mutual understanding.

She desired him, loved him, wanted to *be* with him. But more and more it seemed to her that he resented his feelings for her, that he was only with her because he couldn't stay away.

What kind of marriage would they have? Not a very good one, if things kept on like this.

Two weeks after she accepted Grant's marriage proposal, Steph went into town to run a few errands. She saw Jim Baylis outside the grocery store. He gave her a nod and she nodded back. He looked pretty scruffy, unshaven and not all that clean. She hoped he'd found other work, but no one had called her to ask her about what kind of an employee he'd been.

She almost stopped to ask him how he was

doing, but he turned and walked off before she could say anything, so she just let it be.

Inside, she met up with Lizbeth Stanton in the pasta aisle.

"You're mad at me, aren't you?" Lizbeth demanded. "Just say it. Just admit that you are. I swear to God, I had no clue that you and Grant were a couple. If I had known, I would never have—"

"Lizbeth. I'm not mad. Truly."

"I just want you to know. There was never anything going on between Grant and me. Yeah, I flirted with him, but that was all. It never *went* anywhere."

"It's okay. Really."

"You're sure?"

"Lizbeth, there's no problem, take my word."

"Whew. I hate it when women hate me."

"Well, stop worrying. Because I don't hate you."

"People don't understand. Just because I make no bones about being on the lookout."

"The…lookout?"

"Yeah." She pushed her cart to the side and stepped closer, so no one but Steph would hear. "I'm looking for the right guy. I just want…to get married, you know? Settle down. Have a family. I admit that maybe I kind of hoped Grant might be the one for me. But I promise you, after I saw you and him together the other night…I'd have to be blind not to see that he's Taken. Capital T. And I can respect that, I honestly can."

Steph gave her a big smile. "Well, thank you."

"I hope you'll be real happy together."

"I know we will." The way things were going with her and Grant, Steph knew nothing of the kind. But Lizbeth Stanton didn't need to hear that.

Lizbeth frowned. "Hey. You all right?"

"Yeah. Fine. Really."

Lizbeth trilled out a laugh. "Men. They drive you crazy and break your heart. But you gotta love 'em. I mean, *somebody* has to, right?"

That night, Grant came out to the house for dinner. Over her mother's beef stew, he reported that Jim Baylis had robbed Arletta Hall's gift shop that afternoon. He'd gotten away with the contents of her cash register and what was in her safe, about two thousand dollars altogether. "And when Arletta took too long opening the safe, he shot her in the arm."

"Did they catch him?" asked the new hand.

"Not yet," Grant muttered darkly.

Steph was stunned. "I saw Jim this afternoon. Hanging around outside the Super Save Mart."

"You see him again," Grant said, "you call 911."

Marie put her hand to her throat. "What went wrong with that boy?"

"It's a damn shame," said Rufus. "He seemed like a nice enough guy. Just goes to show you never really know what goes on inside of some folks."

After the meal, the hands went back to the bunkhouse and Steph and Grant sat out on the porch in the summer dark but had nothing to say to each other.

That would have been fine. If only it had been a *good* sort of silence.

But it wasn't. Steph could feel his frustration with her. It came off his big body in waves.

How many times had she tried to bridge this strange gap between them? She only felt close to him when she was in his arms. Though talking about it hadn't worked up till then, she didn't know what else to do.

So she went ahead and gave voice to the issue that always seemed to hang in the air between them. "Rushing to get married isn't going to make everything all right."

"Stalling for months won't, either." He stared out at the shadowed yard. "Unless the real truth is, you never plan to marry me at all."

"I *do* plan to marry you." She felt like she was talking to a stone statue, to a brick wall. "But I want things to be…right between us first."

He turned his head and looked at her then. It was one of those dark, broody looks she got way too many of recently. "There's nothing wrong between us that you can't fix by saying yes now—and meaning it."

She shut her eyes, sucked in a slow breath. "I do mean it."

"So all right, then. Let's—"

"Please, Grant. Don't, okay? Just…don't."

"Fine." He stood. "Listen. I'd better get back to the resort."

She gazed up at him. "What's eating you, Grant Clifton? I really and truly want to understand. But you're just…shut up tight against me and I don't know how to get through."

He made no reply to that, only reached down, took her hand, and hauled her up into his arms. "See you tomorrow night. Come to my rooms."

"I'll be there. You know I will."

He kissed her, kind of slow at first, then more deeply. The kissing, as always, curled her toes and made smoke come out of her ears. If the rest of what they had together could be half as good as the lovemaking, she'd be one contented cowgirl.

Too soon, he was lifting his head. He said goodnight and headed for the Range Rover. She dropped back to the porch step and watched him leave and wondered why she felt so lost and empty inside.

Would she ever get through to him?

She looked down at the toes of her boots and wished she knew where to go from there…

A moment later, she was on her feet. She ran inside to grab her purse and the key to her pickup.

Marie glanced up from the ironing board as she rushed past the open archway to the living room. "Where are you off to, now?"

"I want to see Russ."

"Russ Chilton? Whatever for?"

"Just a visit."

"At nine o'clock at night? It's at least a forty-minute ride to the Flying J."

"Yes, it is. So don't wait up. I'll probably be a couple of hours." She pulled open the door and went through it before Marie could ask another question.

The lights were on in the front room of Russ's white clapboard house when Steph stopped the pickup a few yards from the front walk. Russ must have heard her drive up. He pushed open the door as she mounted the porch steps, the light from within outlining his tall, broad-shouldered frame.

"Steph. What's going on?" The porch light shone on one side of his lean face. He was frowning, probably worried there was some kind of trouble.

Which there was—just not the kind a rancher expects when a neighbor comes calling out of nowhere that time of night. "No problem—I mean, nobody's injured or missing or anything. It's only I…"

He peered at her more closely, brows drawing together. "You okay, Steph?"

"Not really. It's about Grant…"

Without another word, he stepped back and ushered her into the house.

In the kitchen, he offered coffee and she accepted. They sat at the Formica table under the window that, in the daytime, provided a clear view of rolling open land, including both Russ's ranch and the neighboring Hopping H.

Russ set a full mug in front of her and took the chair opposite hers. "So tell me," Grant's longtime best friend said grimly, "he decided he's not ready for marriage, after all? He break your heart, Steph? If he did, I'll be glad to smash that fool's face in for you."

"Oh, Russ. Not…exactly."

Russ sipped his coffee. "Not following. He didn't *exactly* break your heart?"

"He *is* breaking my heart. But not in the way you're thinking."

"Well, then, how?"

"He's…he's mad at me all the time. He wants to run off and get married ASAP. I want to wait a little, get to know him better, as the man I love, you know?"

Russ only frowned and made a motion with his hand that she should tell him more.

"I…want some time before we rush into being husband and wife. I told him I'd marry him in December, but that's just not good enough for him. He's either broody and silent around me, or he's pressuring me to elope, claiming he wants things 'settled' between us—'settled,' he says. At the same time as he won't hardly talk to me. He's not…easy with me, Russ. He used to be my friend, you know?

But that's all gone now. He wants to race off and get married. And when I won't, he's surly as a peeled rattler. I just...sometimes I wonder if he even *likes* me anymore."

"Hell, Steph. He likes you."

"I don't know..."

"He *more* than likes you. Or he wouldn't be after you to marry him, believe me. Not after what he told me when his dad died..."

Steph sat forward in her chair. "What? What did he tell you?"

"He said then that he was never getting married. He said his dad's death almost killed his mom. And he couldn't stand the thought of loving someone so much you'd want to die without them..." Russ looked at the darkened window, though all he could see was their shadowed reflections.

"Go on," she prompted. "What else? Please tell me."

Russ grunted. "You know, he's gonna be mad as hell at me for talking to you about this." He let loose with a rough, low laugh. "But then, it's not like him and me are on the best of terms lately anyway. So here's what I think, for what it's worth.

"Yeah, he's real good at running that resort. He seems to love it. But he's a man carrying around a world of guilt. He promised his dad he'd stick with Clifton's Pride. And he's broken that promise. That's gotta be tough to live with."

Steph jumped to his defense. "But he *has* stuck with Clifton's Pride. For seven years after our dads were killed, he ran the ranch himself, sweated blood over that place. And now he's got *me* to run it for him. And he ended up not being able to bring himself to sell it to that McFarlane woman, even though she offered him a big ol' potfull of money. He's kept his promise to his dad, you know he has."

But Russ shook his head. "Grant's a rancher. He's turned his back on what he is, and that's gotta be bothering him, deep down."

Steph made an impatient sound in her throat. "Oh, come on. He hasn't turned his back on anything. He never liked ranching, he was always itching to get out in the big world. But still, he stuck with it for years after his dad died. Isn't that enough?"

"Uh-uh," said Russ. "You're not getting it."

"No. I get it. I do. But I don't see it. I mean, just because you and I can't imagine enjoying the life Grant has chosen, that doesn't make it wrong for him."

Russ wasn't convinced. "*I* think it's wrong for him. And I keep waiting for the day Grant finally comes to his senses, gives up that fast-track life he's been living and goes back to the ranch where he belongs."

Steph drove away from the Flying J with plenty to think about. In the end, she and Russ had agreed to disagree on the idea that Grant needed, more than anything, to get back to the ranch.

Steph just didn't buy that one. Exactly the opposite, in fact. She happened to be absolutely certain that Grant had finally found the right job for him.

But the guilt angle...

Yeah. Russ might have something there. Grant was the kind of man who kept his word. If he'd promised John Clifton he'd spend his life on Clifton's Pride, well, it would be bound to eat at him that he'd chosen a different path in the end.

And the part about him swearing he'd never get married...

Well, maybe that had something to do with how much trouble he seemed to be having over the idea that he was going to be a married man, after all. And if he feared losing her, well, it kind of made sense that he'd push to get that knot tied right away, to "settle" things between them, the way he kept insisting he wanted them to do.

Maybe, she thought, as she slowed for a sharp curve in the dark highway, she should change her approach here. Maybe she should take the leap and marry him now, do it his way instead of insisting that he do it hers. Maybe she should show a little faith that they were going to work things out in the end, prove to him that she was willing to—

Her thoughts hit a wall as a figure loomed up

out of nowhere in the wash of her headlights. A man. Waving.

She slammed on the brakes, cranking the wheel to the side in order not to run the fool down. Tires screamed as she slid—fishtailing wildly. She turned into the slide.

And by some miracle she managed to regain control. The pickup stopped on the shoulder— facing directly back the way she'd come. Shaking, her mouth tasting of copper, she shifted into Park. After that, she gripped the steering wheel and stared through the windshield at the hard gold glow of her headlights and the darkness beyond.

Well. That had been exciting. *Too* exciting, as a matter of fact.

She blinked. *The man.*

Some guy with a breakdown, most likely, needing help. One of the long list of situations where a person wished she had a cell phone. Too bad that in most of Montana, the things rarely worked.

As her racing heartbeat slowed, she turned to get her rifle off the rack behind the seat. On a deserted highway at night, you just couldn't be too careful.

Before she could pull the weapon down, she heard the tap on the passenger side window. She glanced that way.

And saw Jim Baylis on the other side. He had an automatic pistol pointed at her face.

Chapter Sixteen

"Open this door, Steph." Jim's words were slightly muffled by the glass, but bone-chillingly clear nonetheless.

Her heart gave a thud so heavy, it felt like a fist hitting the wall of her chest. And the taste of pennies was back in her mouth. As fear tried to own her, she considered her options and found them to be severely limited.

Jim tapped the glass again with the gun. "Open it. Lean across nice and slow."

She did as he told her, not sparing so much as a longing glance for her rifle, still in the rack— so close. But totally useless to her without the precious seconds she needed to take it down and load it.

The latch gave, the door swung wide. Jim, smelling of stale sweat and seriously in need of a shave, hitched himself up into the seat and pulled the door shut. He lowered the gun. Now it was aimed at her side.

"Saw you go by an hour ago. Figured at some point, you'd have to come back this way."

Steph said nothing. Really, she couldn't think of anything to say right then that would do her a bit of good.

Jim grunted and wiped his nose on the sleeve of his dirty rawhide jacket. "Piece of crap pickup of mine broke down. So I have to say, I'm real pleased to see you." He tipped his head at the windshield. "Drive."

"Where to?"

"Thunder Canyon Resort. I got me nineteen hundred dollars from old lady Hall's safe. It's not enough. I need some *real* cash, enough for a decent truck, enough to be able to put a lot of miles between me and this town.

"So we're gonna drop in on that rich boyfriend of yours. See how much he's willin' to pay to get his fiancée back."

Twenty minutes later they were rolling up the long private driveway that led to the main lodge, the bright lights of the sprawling, multileveled structure shining up ahead.

Jim leaned across the seat and jabbed her with that gun of his. "Rufus told me Grant's got himself a fancy big apartment on the top floor of the lodge. Ain't that the life?"

Steph said nothing.

Jim laughed. "Where's the key? I heard you and him are engaged. And I know damn well he gave you a key to his place."

Still, she refused to speak, expecting any second to hear the roar of a gunshot echo through the cab, followed instantly by a hot, hard punch to her side that would bloom into agony all too soon.

She thought of her dad, suddenly, so still in the mud with that bullet hole through his head on that rainy day nine years before. Was the same thing going to happen to her?

Apparently not—at least, not right then. Jim grabbed her purse and started rifling through it. He found her wallet, took the sixty-four dollars cash she had in the billfold and then started checking out the sleeves. It only took a few seconds and he was holding up the card key. "What do you know?" He threw the purse on the floor and shoved the money in a pocket. He spotted the sign that pointed the way to underground parking. "Go that way."

She drove around the back of the main building

and into the shorter, downsloping driveway that led into the parking garage. He handed her the key and she stuck it in the key reader. The striped security arm rose. Steph drove inside.

"Park by the elevators."

She found a space not far from the two sets of elevator doors and nosed the pickup into it.

"Turn off the engine and pass me the key to the truck." He didn't ask for the card key—she assumed because he was going to be too busy poking a gun in her ribs to open any doors with it. Opening doors would be her job. "I'll take that fancy diamond ring of yours, too."

Oh, how she longed to spit in his face. But she knew it was a bad time to argue with him. She had to wait for an opening. And with that gun of his pointed straight at her, now wasn't it.

She took off her ring and handed it over.

He shoved it in a pocket of his dirty jeans. "Now, Stephanie," he said. "I'm going to ask some questions and you're going to answer in a truthful way. I don't want to shoot you. It'd be a shame to put a bullet hole through you, especially consider-ing I still got kind of a sweet spot for you, even though you never would give me the time of day. You're a fine lookin' woman and a brave one. But I'll do what I have to do to get what I need. I shot old lady Hall. And I can shoot you. See, I tried to play it straight my whole damn life. But it didn't work out for me. Now I just need cash to get me to someplace where I can start fresh. Understand?"

She nodded.

"One of those elevators over there go straight to the top?"

"No. You have to change elevators on the main floor."

"I was afraid of that." He shrugged out of his jacket, taking his time about it, careful to pass the gun from hand to hand and kept it pointed her way the whole time. He draped the jacket over his arm, masking the gun. "Okay now." He leaned on his door and pushed it open. "Come on toward me. Get out on this side."

She slid across the seat and emerged from the pickup right after him. He shoved the door shut, took her arm and guided her so she was in front of him, kind of tucking the gun against her. To anyone not looking too close, it would appear he was holding her elbow.

"Okay, Steph. Take it nice and easy. Smile and don't make any fast moves."

It all went so smoothly. The elevator opened and two men stepped out. Steph didn't recognize either of them. They nodded, neither man so much as looking twice, and got out of the car.

Jim and Steph got on.

On the main floor, they changed elevators without incident. A bellman recognized her, but only to nod and smile. She nodded back, wanting to scream, knowing if she did, she'd take a bullet for her effort. In no time they were in the second elevator, on their way up.

When the doors slid open on the fifth floor, there was no one in the hall. That was good, right? No one else needed to be hanging around Jim, with his burning need for quick cash and his loaded gun...

"Which one?" Jim demanded.

She stalled, aware of the tiny eye of the security camera, up in the corner, hoping that maybe someone in the security center with its banks of monitors was paying attention.

More than anything, she wanted to keep Grant out of this. There was going to be big trouble—bigger even than the cold, round mouth of the pistol poking into her side—when Grant Clifton saw what Jim Baylis was up to. He would make Jim pay. Which was fine with her—she wanted Jim to pay herself.

But she couldn't bear the thought that Grant might get hurt in the process.

"Which door?" Jim shoved the gun into her side again.

She said, "He might not even be in the suite yet. Sometimes he doesn't get to his rooms until after midnight."

"No problem. I'm willing to wait. Which one?"

"At the end of the hall."

"Let's go."

* * *

Grant sat in the dark in the living room of his suite, an empty whiskey glass at his side. He was thinking about how things change.

How maybe he needed to learn to roll with the punches a little, learn to trust his woman when he knew she deserved his trust. She deserved *everything*. All he could give her, including his sorry, mixed-up heart.

No, he hadn't planned to fall in love.

But hell. It had happened. He loved Steph. And it didn't look like that love would be going away anytime soon. In fact, it was starting to seem to him that he'd *always* loved her. He'd just been too damn stubborn and hardheaded to admit what he felt.

He loved her. He would *be* loving her until the day he died. There was no escaping his love. If he lost her, it would kill him. He'd have to learn to live all over again. Or end up like his mom, walking around with a big old empty hole where his heart used to be.

But, as of now, he *hadn't* lost her. And he wouldn't, not anytime soon, if fate would only smile on them just a little. *And* if he didn't manage to drive her away with his constant insistence that she marry him and do it now...

So maybe, the deal was to learn how to live with loving her, learn how to be a better man than he'd ever thought he'd have to be.

He didn't especially relish crawling on his hands and knees and begging her forgiveness for being a surly jerk in need of a serious attitude adjustment.

But in the end, a man had to do what a man had to do. He knew she was really torn up over him.

Would it be too damn ridiculous to go to her tonight? To ride out to the ranch right now, rouse her from bed, kiss her senseless, swear on the graves of their fathers that he could wait till December, he could do it *her* way, if only she could forgive him for being such an ass?

He shifted to rise. But a muffled, furtive sound from the foyer of the suite had him freezing dead-still where he sat, adrenaline kicking in, lifting the short hairs on the back of his neck.

Steph stuck the card in the slot and pulled it free. The twin lights in the electronic lock blinked green. She turned the handle and the heavy door gave inward. Onto darkness. Through the archway to the living room, she could see the fat, shadowed shapes of expensive, heavily padded sofas and chairs and the big window that was the far wall, framing Thunder Mountain beyond.

Was he here, in his bed? Or safe, for the moment, downstairs in the Lounge or maybe in town at the Hitching Post with the guys?

Oh, dear Lord. Protect him. Somehow, let him be safe...

The desperate man behind her gave her yet another sharp poke with his gun. His sour breath stirred her hair as he put his mouth to her ear.

"No lights." The whisper came, low and soft. And deadly. "No sound. Real slow, we'll have us a good look around." He had the barrel of the gun at the small of her back now, and one hand manacled her arm. "Let's go."

As they tiptoed through the empty living room, then down the hallway on the right to the kitchen and the spare room, the extra bath and Grant's in-suite office, Steph formulated a two-option plan.

If Grant was in his bed, she'd make her move when they entered his bedroom. She'd probably end up taking a bullet. But if she moved fast enough, she should be able to avoid a fatal wound and warn Grant at the same time. Piece of cake.

Yeah. Right.

If the suite was empty, she'd have to wait until Grant came in. She should have a split second when they heard him open the door. An instant when Jim would glance away, distracted by the sound. It would be her chance to dive for cover. And to shout out Grant's name good and loud.

She'd been totally unresisting up till now. That should work in her favor. Jim should be lulled by her obedience, certain she was too scared to take action in her own behalf.

At least, she *hoped* he would be lulled. She had

to admit he didn't *seem* at all overconfident. He moved with careful deliberation. He kept his cool. At every turn, he'd taken pains to keep that gun of his pointed right at her, to keep her close and under his physical control.

He guided her around and they went back along the darkened hallway the way they had come. At each doorway, he pulled her to a halt while he gave the shadowed room they were passing a quick second glance. He was taking nothing for granted. Damn it.

Moving silently and with caution, they crossed the dark living room again and entered the short hall that ended in one door: the door to Grant's bedroom.

The door stood wide-open, darkness beyond. The moon in the wide bedroom window gave just enough light to see that the bed was neatly made. And empty. The door to the bathroom was ajar. It was dark in there, too.

Steph stood in the doorway, staring at that empty bed, her heart knocking hard, at the same time as she felt a weakness in the pit of her stomach: relief. Grant wasn't in the apartment. He was safe for the moment.

And she would be going with option two.

Jim nudged her with the gun again, urging her into the bedroom so he could check things out. She took a step and cleared the threshold.

And all hell broke loose.

Chapter Seventeen

A dark shape erupted from just inside the doorway. Steph ducked instinctively as she heard her captor gasp in surprise. The gun went off, so loud it seemed to rip the air wide-open. A bedside lamp exploded.

The dark shape jumped on Jim.

Grant! Oh, God. Grant.

She was on the floor without knowing how she got there, scooting backward out of the way, as Grant kicked the gun from Jim's hand and took him down.

The men rolled, punching, grunting, punching some more, knocking over tables and sending stuff crashing to the hardwood floor.

The gun!

Steph had seen it spin under the bed. She went for it, flipping to her belly, going flat and sliding under there. She pulled it out and got to her feet as someone started pounding on the door of the suite.

"Security!" a deep voice shouted. How had they gotten here so quickly?

Her stunned mind caught up: Someone must have been watching the monitors in the security center after all.

She heard the door burst open. Two uniformed men ran in, pistols drawn. By then, Grant had the top position. He slammed his fist into Jim's jaw.

Jim groaned. Grant hit him again. And that was when her former kidnapper gave it up. "Hey," he moaned. "All right. It's done, I'm through."

Dawn was breaking over the mountains when they left the sheriff's station after giving their statements. Grant had a gash across the bridge of his nose and his left eye was bright purple, swollen up fat as a hen's egg.

But aside from that, they were both healthy, not a bullet hole in sight. Steph had her engagement diamond back on her ring finger where it belonged.

Grant gave her a smile. Even with the giant shiner, he was the best-looking man in Montana. "What now, my darlin'?"

My darlin'. He said it so easy and sweet. Crazy, but she felt the tears rising.

Must be some strange stress reaction. Now the danger was past, she could let herself go...

With a discreet sniff she told him, "I'd hand over a couple of prime stud bulls for a big cup of coffee, black."

"You got it."

They went to a little coffee shop in New Town. By then, they were both starving. So they took a booth and ordered breakfast.

Steph sipped her coffee and thought how good it tasted. The best coffee she'd ever had. Maybe because she'd made it through the night when for a little while there, she was sure she was a dead woman.

Surviving made the whole world seem brighter, more hopeful, full of beauty.

And love.

She gazed at the man across the booth from her. And the look in his good eye told her that everything was going to be all right between them. "We are going to have us one fine, happy life, Grant Clifton."

One corner of his mouth kicked up in that smile that lit up her world. "You better believe it—and did you call your mom yet?"

She clapped her hand over her mouth. "I completely forgot. She's going to be frantic."

"Phone's back there." He shot a thumb over his shoulder.

The sheriff had returned not only her ring, but also

her wallet and her money, so she grabbed her purse, slid out of the booth and went to make the call.

She probably should have known her mom would have already contacted the sheriff. "They told me what happened," Marie said. "I have to say, I am mightily relieved. They swore to me you were both unhurt…"

"Grant's a little beat up, but it's nothing serious. We're fine, Mom." She cradled the phone gently, let out a soft sigh as she thought of his easy smile, of the way he'd called her *darlin'*. Her heart rose up, light as a sunbeam in her chest. "We're more than fine."

Marie understood. "So. The man who's got everything has learned what he's been missing."

"Yeah. Guess so."

I'm glad for you, honey."

"Oh, Mom. I'm glad, too."

"Love is a rare and fine thing. Treasure it."

"I will, Mom. I swear."

Her Western omelet was waiting when she got back to their table. She slathered it in ketchup and dug in. They ate with gusto, in easy silence.

She thought how she'd never been so happy. Not in her whole twenty-one years of life.

Back in the Range Rover, with her belly full and the danger past, with her future looking extra rosy before her, she let her head droop against the seat rest and closed her eyes.

* * *

"Steph…" His tender voice came to her, luring her to wakefulness.

"Um?"

He kissed her, a gentle brushing of his lips against hers.

She opened her eyes and saw him, right there, so close, his dear face filling her world. "We're here?"

"Yeah. We are."

He'd parked the Range Rover out on open land. She wasn't surprised when she glanced out her side window and saw the rough, jagged outcroppings of bare rock.

The Callister Breaks.

"Oh, Grant." She touched his wonderful beard-stubbled cheek. "It's…fitting. It's right."

"I knew you'd think so. Come on."

They got out of the big vehicle and started walking, hand in hand. It wasn't far. Soon enough they stood above the place where their fathers had died.

"Beautiful here," he said.

"Yeah." She looked out at the rugged beauty of the land, at the wide sky and a hawk, soaring so high above them.

He tugged on her hand and she moved closer, into his strong, warm embrace. He said, "I dream of that day now and then. Of them, dead in the mud. Of how damn brave you were."

She felt a tear rise, spill over and slide down her cheek. "They were fine men."

"The best."

"I suppose I'd better tell you…" She felt suddenly shy. She swiped the tear away, tipped her head down.

He caught her chin and guided it upward so he looked in her eyes again. "Anything. You can tell me anything."

So she did. "After you left last night, I went to the Flying J."

The truly amazing thing was, he instantly knew why. "Hoping Russ could tell you why I'm such a jackass?"

"Oh, more or less. I guess."

"Well. Did he?"

"He helped. Then I kind of thought of it myself. I was just putting together what I would say to you when Jim jumped out into the middle of the road in front of my pickup and I got seriously distracted for the rest of the night."

He laughed. It was a wonderful, free and easy sound. "So now you're safe and here with me, I think you should tell me what you planned to say to me."

She felt shy again. She had to clear her throat before she could begin. "Ahem. I think…you've been afraid to love me. I think it's not what you intended for yourself. I think you had some idea that if you never loved anyone too much, you wouldn't get hurt. Like your poor mom was hurt when your dad was killed."

"Ouch. You got me."

She put her hands on his chest, felt the strong, even beat of his big heart. "Not that it matters anymore, what your problem was with loving. Because all I have to do is look at you to know you've worked it out all by your lonesome."

"Naw. Not by my lonesome. Not by a long shot. You did most of the work, just by being you. By showing me…all I was missing. All I was throwing away."

"But *you* did it. Without me explaining to you what your problem was. You figured it out."

"Yeah. Guess I did."

"Right on time, too."

"Yep. Which is why I was sitting there in the dark, not making a sound, when Jim Baylis brought you to me. At gunpoint."

A chuckle escaped her. "It did work out all right, after all, didn't it?"

"There were a few iffy moments."

"But here we are."

"Oh, yeah," he said. "Together. As we were always meant to be."

"Oh, Grant. I love how you say that."

He dipped his head and kissed her—a quick, sweet one.

When he straightened, she rested her head

against his heart. "Okay," she whispered. "I'm willing now, if you still feel strongly about it. We can get married right away if that's how you want it."

"Hey. Come on. Look at me."

She raised her head. "Yeah?"

"I know. About December. You never dared to say it to me, because I think you knew I couldn't take it. But, Steph. I can take it now."

The tears were rising again. Two of them dribbled down her cheeks. Light as the touch of true love itself, he brushed them away and she asked in a trembling voice, "You're sure?"

He nodded. "You go ahead. You say it right out. We don't need to hide from the past anymore. The past has made us what we are now. The past is part of us. I'm learning that we should no more turn our backs on what came before than we should say no to the future."

She added, "Because we can have both, Grant. I know what you promised your dad. That you'd stick with Clifton's Pride, make him proud by doing right by the land. Well, if you think about it, that's exactly what you *are* doing. You turned the ranch over to me and I'll do what John Clifton wanted, I'll do it with joy in my heart and a smile on my face. And you can go ahead and be a wheeler-dealer golden boy. There's no law that says we both can't live the lives we always wanted."

The wind teased her hair. He guided a few wild

strands behind her ear. "Say it. Out loud. Right here and now. About December."

"It's…when our folks were married. Remember? A double ceremony—Marie and Andre, John and Helen—they said their vows to each other just a few days before Christmas. It's always seemed to me the best time of year for a wedding."

He didn't even hesitate. "December it is, then."

"Oh, Grant. Are you sure?"

"I know what I want now, Steph. You. A lifetime with you. I don't need to rush it now. I don't need to…lock things up. December is fine with me. I can wait."

"Oh, you are just an amazing and wonderful man."

His arms tightened around her. "Prove it. With a kiss."

She lifted her mouth to him and he claimed it. All their passion was in that kiss. All their hope. Their dreams. Their commitment.

Their love.

When he lifted his head, they turned together, to look down at the place where their fathers had died.

She said, "I love you, Grant. I always have."

"I love you, too," he answered. "Always."

Above them, the hawk soared. They heard its wild, hungry cry on the wind. As one, they turned to go home.

To Clifton's Pride. Or his fancy apartment at the resort.

It didn't matter where they went.

Just as long as they were together when they got there.

* * * * *

The new Special Edition continuity
MONTANA MAVERICKS: STRIKING IT RICH
continues in August 2007 with
PAGING DR. RIGHT
by reader favorite Stella Bagwell.
When reluctant heiress Mia Smith meets
Marshall Cates, she senses that
he could mend more than broken bones.
But will the handsome doctor still
want her when he discovers how
she came into her money?
Available wherever Silhouette Books are sold.

Every Life Has More
Than One Chapter

Award-winning author Stevi Mittman delivers
another hysterical mystery, featuring Teddi
Bayer, an irrepressible heroine, and her to-
die-for hero, Detective Drew Scoones. After
all, life on Long Island can be murder!

*Turn the page for a sneak peek
at the warm and funny fourth book,
WHOSE NUMBER IS UP, ANYWAY?,
in the Teddi Bayer series,
by STEVI MITTMAN.
On sale August 7.*

"Before redecorating a room, I always advise
my clients to empty it of everything but one
chair. Then I suggest they move that chair
from place to place, sitting in it, until the
placement feels right. Trust your instincts
when deciding on furniture placement. Your
room should 'feel right.'"

—TipsFromTeddi.com

Gut feelings. You know, that gnawing in the pit of
your stomach that warns you that you are about to
do the absolute stupidest thing you could do?
Something that will ruin life as you know it?

I've got one now, standing at the butcher counter
in King Kullen, the grocery store in the same strip
mall as L.I. Lanes, the bowling alley cum billiard
parlor I'm in the process of redecorating for its
"Grand Opening."

I realize being in the wrong supermarket probably doesn't sound exactly dire to you, but you

aren't the one buying your father a brisket at a store your mother will somehow know isn't Waldbaum's.

And then, June Bayer isn't your mother.

The woman behind the counter has agreed to go into the freezer to find a brisket for me, since there aren't any in the case. There are packages of pork tenderloin, piles of spareribs and rolls of sausage, but no briskets.

Warning Number Two, right? I should be so out of here.

But no, I'm still in the same spot when she comes back out, brisketless, her face ashen. She opens her mouth as if she is going to scream, but only a gurgle comes out.

And then she pinballs out from behind the counter, knocking bottles of Peter Luger Steak Sauce to the floor on her way, now hitting the tower of cans at the end of the prepared foods aisle and sending them sprawling, now making her way down the aisle, careening from side to side as she goes.

Finally, from a distance, I hear her shout, "He's deeeeeeaaaad! Joey's deeeeeaaaad."

My first thought is *You should always trust your gut*.

My second thought is that now, somehow, my mother will know I was in King Kullen. For weeks I will have to hear "What did you expect?" as though whenever you go to King Kullen someone turns up dead. And if the detective investigating the case turns out to be Detective Drew Scoones…well, I'll never hear the end of that from her, either.

She still suspects I murdered the guy who was found dead on my doorstep last Halloween just to get Drew back into my life.

Several people head for the butcher's freezer and I position myself to block them. If there's one thing I've learned from finding people dead—and the guy on my doorstep wasn't the first one—it's that the police get very testy when you mess with their murder scenes.

"You can't go in there until the police get here," I say, stationing myself at the end of the butcher's counter and in front of the Employees Only door, acting as if I'm some sort of authority. "You'll contaminate the evidence if it turns out to be murder."

Shouts and chaos. You'd think I'd know better than to throw the word *murder* around. Cell phones are flipping open and tongues are wagging.

I amend my statement quickly. "Which, of course, it probably isn't. Murder, I mean. People die all the time, and it's not always in hospitals or their own beds, or…" I babble when I'm nervous, and the idea of someone dead on the other side of the freezer door makes me very nervous.

So does the idea of seeing Drew Scoones again. Drew and I have this on-again, off-again sort of thing…that I kind of turned off.

Who knew he'd take it so personally when he tried to get serious and I responded by saying we could talk about *us* tomorrow—and then caught a plane to my parents' condo in Boca the next day? In July. In the middle of a job.

For some crazy reason, he took that to mean that I was avoiding him and the subject of *us*.

That was three months ago. I haven't seen him since.

The manager, who identifies himself and points to his nameplate in case I don't believe him, says he has to go into *his cooler*. "Maybe Joey's not dead," he says. "Maybe he can be saved, and you're letting him die in there. Did you ever think of that?"

In fact, I hadn't. But I had thought that the murderer might try to go back in to make sure his tracks were covered, so I say that I will go in and check.

Which means that the manager and I couple up and go in together while everyone pushes against the doorway to peer in, erasing any chance of finding clean prints on that Employee Only door.

I expect to find carcasses of dead animals hanging from hooks, and maybe Joey hanging from one, too. I think it's going to be very creepy and I steel myself, only to find a rather benign series of shelves with large slabs of meat laid out carefully on them, along with boxes and boxes marked simply Chicken.

Nothing scary here, unless you count the body

of a middle-aged man with graying hair sprawled faceup on the floor. His eyes are wide open and unblinking. His shirt is stiff. His pants are stiff. His body is stiff. And his expression, you should forgive the pun—is frozen. Bill-the-manager crosses himself and stands mute while I pronounce the guy dead in a sort of *happy now?* tone.

"We should not be in here," I say, and he nods his head emphatically and helps me push people out of the doorway just in time to hear the police sirens and see the cop cars pull up outside the big store windows.

Bobbie Lyons, my partner in Teddi Bayer Interior Designs (and also my neighbor, my best friend and my private fashion police), and Mark, our carpenter (and my dogsitter, confidant, and ego booster), rush in from next door. They beat the cops by a half step and shout out my name. People point in my direction.

After all the publicity that followed the unfortunate incident during which I shot my ex-husband, Rio Gallo, and then the subsequent murder of my first client—which I solved, I might add—it seems like the whole world, or at least all of Long Island, knows who I am.

Mark asks if I'm all right. (Did I remember to mention that the man is drop-dead-gorgeous-but-a-decade-too-young-for-me-yet-too-old-for-my-daughter-thank-god?) I don't get a chance to answer him because the police are quickly closing in on the store manager and me.

"The woman—" I begin telling the police. Then I have to pause for the manager to fill in her name, which he does: *Fran*.

I continue. "Right. Fran. Fran went into the freezer to get a brisket. A moment later she came out and screamed that Joey was dead. So I'd say she was the one who discovered the body."

"And you are…" the cop asks me. It comes out a bit like who do I *think* I am, rather than who am I really?

"An innocent bystander," Bobbie, hair perfect, makeup just right, says, carefully placing her body between the cop and me.

"And she was just leaving," Mark adds. They each take one of my arms.

Fran comes into the inner circle surrounding the cops. In case it isn't obvious from the hairnet and bloodstained white apron with Fran embroidered on it, I explain that she was the butcher who was going for the brisket. Mark and Bobbie take that as a signal that I've done my job and they can now get me out of there. They twist around, with me in the middle, as if we're a Rockettes line, until we are facing away from the butcher counter. They've managed to propel me a few steps toward the exit when disaster—in the form of a Mazda RX7 pulling up at the loading curb—strikes.

Mark's grip on my arm tightens like a vise. "Too late," he says.

Bobbie's expletive is unprintable. "Maybe there's a back door," she suggests, but Mark is right. It's too late.

I've laid my eyes on Detective Scoones. And while my gut is trying to warn me that my heart shouldn't go there, regions farther south are melting at just the sight of him.

"Walk," Bobbie orders me.

And I try to. Really.

Walk, I tell my feet. *Just put one foot in front of the other.*

I can do this because I know, in my heart of hearts, that if Drew Scoones was still interested in me, he'd have gotten in touch with me after I returned from Boca. And he didn't.

Since he's a detective, Drew doesn't have to wear one of those dark blue Nassau County Police uniforms. Instead, he's got on jeans, a tight-fitting T-shirt and a tweedy sports jacket. If you think that sounds good, you should see him. Chiseled features, cleft chin, brown hair that's naturally a little sandy in the front, a smile that…well, that doesn't matter. He isn't smiling now.

He walks up to me, tucks his sunglasses into his breast pocket and looks me over from head to toe.

"Well, if it isn't Miss Cut and Run," he says. "Aren't you supposed to be somewhere in Florida or something?" He looks at Mark accusingly, as if he was covering for me when he told Drew I was gone.

"Detective Scoones?" one of the uniforms says. "The stiff's in the cooler and the woman who found him is over there." He jerks his head in Fran's direction.

Drew continues to stare at me.

You know how when you were young, your mother always told you to wear clean underwear in case you were in an accident? And how, a little further on, she told you not to go out in hair rollers because you never knew who you might see—or who might see you? And how now your best friend says she wouldn't be caught dead without makeup and suggests you shouldn't, either?

Okay, today, *finally,* in my overalls and Converse sneakers, I get it.

I brush my hair out of my eyes. "Well, I'm back," I say. As if he hasn't known my exact whereabouts. The man is a detective, for heaven's sake. "Been back awhile."

Bobbie has watched the exchange and apparently decided she's given Drew all the time he deserves. "And we've got work to do, so…" she says, grabbing my arm and giving Drew a little two-fingered wave goodbye.

As I back up a foot or two, the store manager sees his chance and places himself in front of Drew, trying to get his attention. Maybe what makes Drew such a good detective is his ability to focus.

Only what he's focusing on is me.

"Phone broken? Carrier pigeon died?" he asks me, taking in Fran, the manager, the meat counter and that Employees Only door, all without taking his eyes off me.

Mark tries to break the spell. "We've got work to do there, you've got work to do here, Scoones," Mark says to him, gesturing toward next door. "So it's back to the alley for us."

Drew's lip twitches. "You working the alley now?" he says.

"If you'd like to follow me," Bill-the-manager, clearly exasperated, says to Drew—who doesn't respond. It's as if waiting for my answer is all he has to do.

So, fine. "You knew I was back," I say.

The man has known my whereabouts every hour of the day for as long as I've known him. And my mother's not the only one who won't buy that he "just happened" to answer this particular call. In fact, I'm willing to bet my children's lunch money that he's taken every call within ten miles of my home since the day I got back.

And now he's gotten lucky.

"*You* could have called *me*," I say.

"You're the one who said *tomorrow* for our talk and then flew the coop, chickie," he says. "I figured the ball was in your court."

"Detective?" the uniform says. "There's something you ought to see in here."

Drew gives me a look that amounts to *in or out?*

He could be talking about the investigation, or about our relationship.

Bobbie tries to steer me away. Mark's fists are balled. Drew waits me out, knowing I won't be able to resist what might be a murder investigation.

Finally he turns and heads for the cooler.

And, like a puppy dog, I follow.

Bobbie grabs the back of my shirt and pulls me to a halt.

"I'm just going to show him something," I say, yanking away.

"Yeah," Bobbie says, pointedly looking at the buttons on my blouse. The two at breast level have popped. "That's what I'm afraid of."

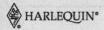

REQUEST YOUR FREE BOOKS!
2 FREE NOVELS PLUS 2 FREE GIFTS!

Silhouette®

SPECIAL EDITION®
Life, Love and Family!

YES! Please send me 2 FREE Silhouette Special Edition® novels and my 2 FREE gifts. After receiving them, if I don't wish to receive any more books, I can return the shipping statement marked "cancel." If I don't cancel, I will receive 6 brand-new novels every month and be billed just $4.24 per book in the U.S., or $4.99 per book in Canada, plus 25¢ shipping and handling per book and applicable taxes, if any*. That's a savings of at least 15% off the cover price! I understand that accepting the 2 free books and gifts places me under no obligation to buy anything. I can always return a shipment and cancel at any time. Even if I never buy another book from Silhouette, the two free books and gifts are mine to keep forever.   235 SDN EEYU   335 SDN EEY6

Name _____ (PLEASE PRINT) _____

Address _____ Apt. _____

City _____ State/Prov. _____ Zip/Postal Code _____

Signature (if under 18, a parent or guardian must sign)

Mail to the **Silhouette Reader Service™:**
IN U.S.A.: P.O. Box 1867, Buffalo, NY 14240-1867
IN CANADA: P.O. Box 609, Fort Erie, Ontario L2A 5X3
Not valid to current Silhouette Special Edition subscribers.

Want to try two free books from another line?
Call 1-800-873-8635 or visit www.morefreebooks.com.

* Terms and prices subject to change without notice. NY residents add applicable sales tax. Canadian residents will be charged applicable provincial taxes and GST. This offer is limited to one order per household. All orders subject to approval. Credit or debit balances in a customer's account(s) may be offset by any other outstanding balance owed by or to the customer. Please allow 4 to 6 weeks for delivery.

Your Privacy: Silhouette is committed to protecting your privacy. Our Privacy Policy is available online at www.eHarlequin.com or upon request from the Reader Service. From time to time we make our lists of customers available to reputable firms who may have a product or service of interest to you. If you would prefer we not share your name and address, please check here. ☐

SSE07

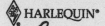

HARLEQUIN®

Super Romance®

*Looking for a romantic, emotional
and unforgettable escape?*

*You'll find it this month and every month
with a Harlequin Superromance!*

Rory Gorenzi has a sense of humor and a sense of
honor. She also happens to be good with children.

Seamus Lee, widower and father of four, needs
someone with exactly those traits.

They meet at the Colorado mountain school owned
by Rory's father, where she teaches skiing and
avalanche safety. But Seamus—and his children—
learn more from her than that....

Look for

GOOD WITH CHILDREN

by Margot Early,

*available August 2007, and these other
fantastic titles from Harlequin Superromance.*

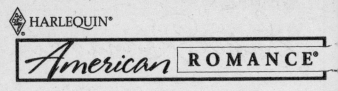

HARLEQUIN®

American **ROMANCE**®

TEXAS LEGACIES: THE CARRIGANS

Get to the Heart of a Texas Family

WITH

THE RANCHER NEXT DOOR
by
Cathy Gillen Thacker

She'll Run The Ranch—And Her Life—Her Way!

On her alpaca ranch in Texas, Rebecca encounters
constant interference from Trevor McCabe, the
bossy rancher next door. Rebecca becomes very
friendly with Vince Owen, her other neighbor and
Trevor's archrival from college. Trevor's problem
is convincing Rebecca that he is on her side, and
aware of Vince's ulterior motives. But Trevor has
fallen for her in the process….

On sale July 2007

SILHOUETTE

SPECIAL EDITION™

Look for

THE BILLIONAIRE NEXT DOOR

by Jessica Bird

For Wall Street hotshot Sean O'Banyon, going home to south Boston brought back bad memories. But Lizzie Bond, his father's sweet, girl-next-door caretaker, was there to ease the pain. It was instant attraction—until Sean found out she was named sole heir, and wondered what her motives really were....

THE O'BANYON BROTHERS

On sale August 2007.

SPECIAL EDITION

#1843 PAGING DR. RIGHT—Stella Bagwell
Montana Mavericks: Striking It Rich

Mia Smith came to Thunder Canyon Resort for some peace and quiet, but with her recent inheritance, other guests took her for a wealthy socialite and wouldn't leave her be. At least she found comfort with the resort's handsome staff doctor Marshall Cates, but would her painful past and humble beginnings nip their budding romance?

#1844 THE BILLIONAIRE NEXT DOOR—Jessica Bird
The O'Banyon Brothers

For Wall Street hot shot Sean O'Banyon, going home to South Boston after his abusive father's death brought back miserable memories. But Lizzie Bond, his father's sweet, girl-next-door caretaker, was there to ease the pain. It was instant attraction—and then Sean found out she was named sole heir, and he began to wonder what her motives really were....

#1845 REMODELING THE BACHELOR—Marie Ferrarella
The Sons of Lily Moreau

Son of a famous, though flighty artist, Philippe Zabelle had grown up to be a set-in-his-ways bachelor. Yet when the successful software developer hired J. D. Wyatt to do some home repairs, something clicked. J.D. was a single mother with a flair for fixing anything… even Philippe's long-broken heart.

#1846 THE COWBOY AND THE CEO—Christine Wenger
She was city. He was country. But on a trip to a Wyoming ranch that made disabled children's dreams come true, driven business owner Susan Collins fell hard for caring cowboy Clint Skully. Having been left at the altar once before, would Clint risk the farm on love this time around?

#1847 ACCIDENTALLY EXPECTING—Michelle Celmer
In one corner, attorney Miranda Reed, who wrote the definitive guide to divorce and the modern woman. In the other, Zackery Jameson, staunch supporter of traditional family values. When these polar opposites sparred on a radio talk show, neither yielded any ground. So how did it come to pass that Miranda was now expecting Zack's baby?

#1848 A FAMILY PRACTICE—Gayle Kasper
After personal tragedy struck, Dr. Luke Phillips took off on a road trip. But when he crashed his motorcycle in the Arizona desert, it was local holistic healer Mariah Cade who got him to stop running. Whether it was in her tender touch or her gentle way with her daughter, Mariah was the miracle cure for all that ailed the good doctor.